Large Print Western BOWIE S
Bowie, Sam, 1903-19
Thunderhead range
[text (large print)]

THUNDERHEAD
RANGE

Center Point
Large Print

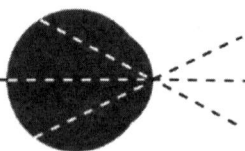

**This Large Print Book carries the
Seal of Approval of N.A.V.H.**

THUNDERHEAD RANGE

Sam Bowie

CENTER POINT LARGE PRINT
THORNDIKE, MAINE

This Center Point Large Print edition
is published in the year 2018 by arrangement with
Golden West Literary Agency.

First US edition: Monarch Books

The text of this Large Print edition is unabridged.
In other aspects, this book may vary
from the original edition.
Printed in the United States of America
on permanent paper.
Set in 16-point Times New Roman type.

ISBN: 978-1-64358-032-6 (hardcover)
ISBN: 978-1-64358-036-4 (paperback)

Library of Congress Cataloging-in-Publication Data

Names: Bowie, Sam, 1903-1980, author.
Title: Thunderhead range / Sam Bowie.
Description: Center Point Large Print edition. | Thorndike, Maine :
    Center Point Large Print, 2018.
Identifiers: LCCN 2018041780| ISBN 9781643580326
    (hardcover : alk. paper) | ISBN 9781643580364 (pbk. : alk. paper)
Subjects: LCSH: Large type books. | GSAFD: Western stories.
Classification: LCC PS3503.A5575 T49 2018 | DDC 813/.52—dc23
LC record available at https://lccn.loc.gov/2018041780

THUNDERHEAD
RANGE

CHAPTER ONE

Old Coke was drunk the night Les Parson died. The stone jug he steadied between his booted feet as the buckboard jounced over the ruts of the Tapline road was now less than a third full, and his red-rimmed eyes surveyed the moonlit land with the owlish intensity of a man who, realizing that his senses are slightly impaired, strives by sheer will power to orient his reeling mind.

For this reason he refused to believe his eyesight when he noticed the figure huddled under the slicker—a dark patch in the middle of the road.

But the team had not even sniffed Old Coke's jug. They saw the body and shied sidewise so that one of the wheels struck the sharp edge of rock outcropping and broke, and the pole between them snapped.

Old Coke was thrown out, making a spidery arc in the dark air and landing on his head. Even afterward he maintained that, had he not been drunk at the time, the fall would have killed him.

As it was, he struggled upright, cursing, and scowled at the team which had run the shattered buckboard into a pole pine and now stood hopelessly entangled in the wreckage of the harness.

Three hours later Coke walked lamely into the yard of the home ranch at Thunderhead and sent his wild high cry echoing back from the sharp cliff of the hills behind the ranch.

A light flared in the bunkhouse. The foreman thrust his yellow head out of the door. "Stop that racket, you souse, or I'll give you something to yell about."

Old Coke was no longer drunk and his dark, heavy hair was matted where blood from the cut in his scalp had oozed out.

"It's Les," he called. "He's laying in the road. He's got a hole in the back of his head."

"What's that?" King Parson had come onto the porch of the main house, the moonlight rich on his heavy body, showing that he wore nothing but his undershirt.

Coke stopped and turned that way, going forward in a rubber-legged fashion to tell his story.

"Les was in the middle of the road. Someone had thrown his slicker over him, but his horse was gone and he'd been shot in the back of his head."

It was Jacoby, the foreman, who brought Les's body in, and a group of silent, angry men who later gathered in the front room of the ranch house. Of the group King Parson was the least affected. Actually he had had small love for his dead son. The boy had been too like his father.

The Parsons could not tolerate any authority over them, and his sons were the only beings whom King had never been able to browbeat into obedience.

King Parson was a man so utterly self-centered that the average human relationships touched him hardly at all. Anyone who had ever stood in his way had suffered for it, and now not even Les was an exception.

But even King had the common sense to put on a show of feeling before his crew. They were hard-bitten men, schooled in violence, without consciences or morals, but family ties are the strongest bond in the human race and unless King pretended a grief he did not sense they would have looked at him suspiciously, doubting his loyalty as far as they were concerned.

And he knew from experience that this loyalty, this willingness to blindly follow the orders of the owner of their ranch was his sole protection, his sole shield against a hostile valley around him.

So he stood over his dead son, his red, weathered face ugly beneath three days' growth of beard, and swore in a bitter voice.

"Someone got mighty close." He was looking at the spot where the powder flash had burned the hair and left its pitted marks upon the surrounding skin. "This wasn't a fight. This was murder."

The crew watched him, satisfied with his show

of rage. His blue eyes, pale as skimmed milk, considered the dead boy but his anger didn't penetrate below the surface of his features. Actually he felt more relief than he had in weeks.

The next morning they were burying Les in the tiny cemetery behind the west pasture when Dale Thorne rode into the yard. Had he planned it, Dale could not have chosen a worse moment for his homecoming, for there had never been anything but hatred between his stepfather and himself.

Dale saw the crowd around the grave and walked up the slight rise. King watched him come without change of expression. Nothing was said between the two men until the last shovel full of dirt had been dumped on top of the plain box.

Later, when Dale faced his stepfather in the long room which had been his mother's pride but which was now dirty, littered with gear, its table scarred with spur marks, he made no effort to keep the bitterness from his tone.

"You might at least clean the place up once in awhile. It looks like pigs live here."

King Parson poured himself a drink from the bottle which rested on the table between a broken cinch and a fancy bridle.

"No one asked you to come back. If you don't like the way I run Thunderhead, stay away until I die."

Dale said savagely, "It's a shame it wasn't you instead of Les that Coke found in the road."

King mocked him. "You would have loved that, wouldn't you? With me dead you could have come back to a third interest in the biggest ranch in the country. Maybe you thought it was me instead of Les. We're about the same size, and in the moonlight we would look much the same. I suppose you can prove where you were last night?"

Thorne was as tall as his stepfather but thirty pounds lighter. Not that there was a pound of fat on King Parson. The man was built like a block of granite, and although he was forty-five he was still the strongest man in the valley.

But his face was no tighter than Thorne's at the moment. Dale's face was thin, a little gaunt from much riding, with a hint of Indian ancestry in the highness of his cheekbones, and now he made no attempt to mask his anger and disgust.

"If you're suggesting that I shot Les you're crazy."

"Someone did." King's tone still held its touch of mockery. "You've been gone three years. No one has heard a single word from you. Suddenly you ride in here, the morning after Les is murdered."

Dale Thorne spoke steadily as his dark eyes met Parson's pale blue ones, "Les was a spoiled kid, nearly as spoiled as Ford. I've whaled him before

11

and I might have tried to whale him again if he got out of line, but he was my mother's son, and, therefore, my brother. Blood means something to me, King. You were always prattling about blood, and how wonderful it was to be a Parson. But you hated Les from the time he could walk. You hated Ford. You hated them almost as much as you did me."

Parson did not appear to hear. "Someone killed Les and when I find out who I'll make him sorry he was ever born."

"That I don't doubt." The younger man had not moved from his place beside the table. He stood stiff, ready like a coiled spring—a stranger in this room that had been a part of his childhood, a stranger on the ranch which his father had carved from the wilderness, knowing that he was unwelcome, knowing that King would love nothing better than to kill him, trying to goad the man before him into attempting just that.

"You have the ability to make everyone hate you. There isn't a man or woman or child in the valley or in the hills who wouldn't gladly cut your throat."

"Cattle." King poured himself another drink. "Coyotes who run with their tails between their legs when I ride by." He tossed off the drink. "Since you don't like me and I don't like you, why in hell did you come back?"

"To get my ranch."

"Your ranch?"

Dale spoke in a low voice. "My ranch. Oh, I know, my mother willed it to you for life when she died, with the proviso that it come to my brothers and me at your death. But in California I learned something I had not known before. The ranch was never my mother's to will. My father left it to *me*."

King set his glass carefully on the battered table. "I suppose you talked to DuBois?"

"I did."

"Look," said Parson, and he sounded more friendly than at any time since Dale's arrival. "That's an old story. DuBois tried to sell it to me the year Martha died. He threatened to go to the court and swear that your father drew a will the day before he died, leaving the ranch to you. I told him to produce the will. He couldn't. He wanted ten thousand dollars. I ran him out of the country."

Dale did not answer and the older man was thoughtful for several minutes. "Les's death changes things. All Ford can think of is women and gambling. Stay at the ranch. Help me. It will be yours and Ford's someday."

Dale stayed silent, wondering what was going on in King Parson's active mind behind the opacity of the pale, expressionless eyes.

King Parson had never asked for help, or wanted it, in his whole life, and Dale knew that he wanted none now. The offer might be prompted by one of two desires. King might honestly believe that Dale had had something to do with his half-brother's death, might be using this means of making certain of Dale's presence in the country while Les's murder was investigated.

Or it might be that the talk of another will, signed by Dale's father, leaving the ranch to Dale rather than to his mother, worried King Parson more than he was willing to admit. Perhaps, he wanted to keep the younger man where he could watch him.

Dale shook his head. "Sorry, King. It won't work. I've never liked you, and you've never liked me."

Parson poured a second drink. "No. I don't like you. You're too much like your father. You're soft, and I have no use for soft people."

"Maybe I've changed," Dale said. "I'm warning you, I'm going to look into this will story, and if I find there's anything to it I'll throw you off Thunderhead as fast as I can."

"Do that." Parson laughed suddenly. "Do that, but when you come riding in bring a few guns with you. It won't be easy."

He walked to the door as Dale crossed the yard. Old Coke was standing beside the cook shack, his mouth split in a nearly toothless grin.

"Hey, Bronco!"

Dale stopped. His face, which had been stern

in its harshness, loosened. A moment later he had Old Coke by the shoulders, spinning him around like a barrel-sized top.

"You old rustler. I thought you'd drunk yourself to death years ago."

The cook was beaming. "They ain't made the liquor Old Coke can't handle. You home to stay, boy?"

"I'm home, but not to stay here."

The humor went out of Coke's face, leaving it old and sagging. "Things ain't like they used to be." He spat thoughtfully in the dust between his booted feet. "They ain't never been the same since your daddy died." He glanced around and saw King Parson watching him from the porch.

"The old riders are gone. I'd be gone myself if there was any place for a broken down man to go. Watch yourself, Bronco. This is a gun crew now. They're mean."

Dale nodded. "As soon as I light you're coming with me."

The wizened face twisted and Dale Thorne thought the old man was going to cry. It hurt him deeply. After his father's death, after his mother had married King Parson, it had been Coke who took an interest in him; Coke who taught him to ride, to shoot; Coke who had never been too busy to listen to his complaints.

"You mean that, Dale?"

"I mean it." He gripped Coke's shoulder and

15

shook it gently, then moved on to his horse.

Coke stood watching him ride out of the yard, not conscious that King Parson had left the porch and was coming up behind him until the ranch owner said,

"You like it here, Coke?"

The old cook spun, his expression changing, becoming defensive, indrawn. "Why, sure."

"I just wanted to know. Damn a man who isn't loyal to his brand."

He grinned as Coke scuttled into the cook shack like a frightened crab. It pleased the sadistic side of King Parson's nature to know that people were afraid of him. He stood a moment longer, staring out toward the road. Already Dale Thorne was climbing the saddle which marked the eastern end of the valley, a figure dimmed by distance.

Parson turned finally and walked to the blacksmith shop where Mark Jacoby, his foreman, was overseeing the shoeing of a horse. He motioned and Jacoby joined him, a big man with a wide chest under his grimy shirt.

"See your stepson showed up," Jacoby stated.

Parson did not answer directly. "Pick out one of the men Dale doesn't know. Fire him. Send him into Climax and tell him to keep a watch on Dale. He can give his messages to Joe Blonk at the Last Chance. We'll pick them up there."

The foreman considered him thoughtfully. "What are you going to do?"

16

King Parson savored his answer before he gave it. "Maybe nothing. Maybe we'll hang him. It depends on what the sheriff learns about Les's death."

CHAPTER TWO

Climax lay in a fold of the foothills like a man sleeping sprawled against a wall. To the south and east the contour of the land fell away in ripples, while at the north end of the valley high ridges pinched in so that there was hardly room for the hurrying stream and the twisting roadway following its tortured course.

Dale Thorne came through this pass late in the afternoon, checking his horse at the crest for a long look at the town he had always considered home.

It was seventeen miles by trail from Thunderhead to the spatter of log buildings making up the town. Yet the big ranch had always dominated Climax as it dominated the surrounding country.

He urged the tired horse onward, dropping down the gentle grade of the main street, stopping before the slanting hitch rack of the Climax House, swinging down from the saddle heavy with weariness.

It was, he realized, as he loosened the slicker wrapped blanket roll from behind the worn saddle, three full years since he had ridden out of this community, vowing never to return.

He had been twenty-one then, resentful of his mother's death, of the unquestioned domination of his stepfather, and he had hated the merchants of Climax for knuckling under to King Parson almost as thoroughly as he hated Parson himself.

He fastened the horse and with the bed roll under his arm crossed the slatted sidewalk, climbed the three steps, crossed the gallery and came into the long, narrow, darkish lobby.

A bell rested on the high desk beside the open stairway leading upward to the second floor corridor. He hit it and waited, his eyes unseeing on the key board with its rows of pegs supporting the heavy brass keys.

At a sound from the dining room door he turned his head, and heard Clara Austin say, "Bronc," in a surprised voice.

She was no more surprised than he. He let the bed roll slide from under his arm and took half a step forward. "Why, Clara."

When he had ridden out she had been a leggy girl of fifteen with hair that floated behind her like a red cloud in the breeze as she spurred her horse up Climax's streets.

Now she was a woman, her legs concealed by the sweep of her gray dress, her hair caught in a soft knot at the nape of her slender neck, the freckles which had once sprayed across the slightly short nose now just barely discernible beneath the opalescence of her clear skin.

Only her eyes were the same, gray-green,

holding quick lights that came and went with the swift change of her inner thoughts.

"Where did you drop from?"

He said, "The long trail. I've seen lots of country in the last three years. Texas, Mexico, California."

"Then why did you come back?" There was something in her tone he did not understand—a hard note of rebellion, of dissatisfaction, of discontent.

Why had he come back? Because a dying man had told him about a will which had probably never existed, because in three years of wandering he had failed to find the elusive peace he sought, because he was constantly driven by an urge hard to put into words—an urge to recapture that which in his own mind was rightfully his.

"This is my country." He said it simply, for it was a simple thing. Here lay his roots, in the rocky soil of the rising hills, in the lush parks and bottoms whose grass was unequaled any place in the world, in the valley under the frowning stone face which men had named Thunderhead and from which the ranch had taken its identity.

"You're a fool," she said. She stepped behind the desk and turned the ledger which had served the hotel as a register for twenty years, marred with the cramped, ink-blotted signatures of the straying men who had at one time or another wandered through the town. "There's nothing here to hold anyone."

He picked up the pen and signed his name. "You don't sound happy."

She looked at him, her full lips pouting a little. "What is there to be happy about? My uncle died last year and left me this. . . ." She indicated the dark lobby with a wave of her hand. "Isn't that something for a woman to look forward to, running a third rate hotel in a flea-bitten cattle town?"

"You could get married."

She had been reaching for a key. "That's just what I intend to do. You probably haven't been back long enough to hear. I'm going to be your sister-in-law."

"You're marrying Ford?"

Her upper lip curled. "Ford's an ass."

The thought struck him hard. "You don't mean Les?"

"And why not? What's wrong with Les?"

He realized then with sickening certainty that she had not heard of Les's death, that the news had not even reached the town. It was like King Parson. The man kept his own counsel, and as he put it, usually killed his own snakes. He would not report the murder to the sheriff until it served his purpose to do so.

But it left Dale in a terrible spot, that of being forced to tell the girl that Les was dead.

He spoke slowly. "I don't know how to say this, to soften the fact for you, but I think you ought to know."

Her tone was a little mocking. "Don't tell me Les has another girl, or that he's married already."

"I'm afraid it's worse than that."

"Worse . . . ?"

"I just came from the ranch. Les is dead, Clara."

She watched him, her green eyes widening as if she more than half suspected that he was not telling the truth, that this was some kind of grizzly joke. "Dead . . . he can't be dead. Why, I saw Ford this morning. Ford didn't say anything about it."

"Ford probably doesn't know. Old Coke found Les last night in the trail. He had been shot in the back of the head."

Clara swayed, grasping at the edge of the desk for support. She stood as if the news had numbed her, making her oblivious of passing time. "Dead." The word was a sigh. Suddenly she began to cry.

Dale Thorne was uncertain what to do. He did not know much about women. During his childhood his mother had been too occupied with her younger sons, with her new husband, to spend time with him.

He had lived for the most part in the bunkhouse, raised by Old Coke and the crew, and during the years of his wandering he had had little contact with the other sex.

"Take it easy, Clara. I know it's tough, but things like this happen, and . . ."

She stumbled blindly around the end of the desk. She came to him as if not knowing quite what she did, and his arms opened automatically to receive her.

"Oh, Les." Her face butted into his shoulder and her arms went about him, the tense, nervous fingers biting into his shirt.

He held her tightly, feeling convulsive shudders run through her slim body. "What will I do now? What will I do?"

He had no answer, but he knew a sudden protectiveness which he had never experienced before. "It will work out." He stooped then and pressed his lips against the dampness of her cheek. "It will work out. Everything does."

Later, in the narrow room with its sagging, sway-backed bed, its washstand and dresser, he stood before the clouded mirror considering what had happened in the last few hours. Before, Clara Austin had been only another girl, a tomboy growing up, but in his eyes a child.

She was a child no longer. He could still feel the pressure of her young arms as they had circled him, and the memory brought a hotness to his cheeks.

There was no real reason, he thought, why he

should feel responsible for her except, perhaps, that he was the brother of the man she had planned to marry, but he did feel that he should look after her.

He stripped off his shirt. The room was still warm from the heat of the day although the sun was already far down. The water in the pitcher was tepid, yet it felt cooling to his skin as he washed the trail grime from his body.

Finished, he found a clean shirt in the bed roll and dressed. Then he hesitated. The single gun, its belt and worn holster, lay on the bed where he had tossed it when he first came in. As a boy he had never worn a gun in Climax, but now he lifted it, fastening the scarred buckle so that the holster hung flat against his lean hip.

It was, he thought, a kind of symbol of his new position, of the thing he planned to do, for never in memory had he seen King Parson ride without a gun at his belt.

Dale went down the empty stairs and crossed the lobby. Sounds from the kitchen beyond the dining room told that supper was already being prepared. There was no sight of Clara, no one in the lobby.

The sheriff's office was in one corner of the frame courthouse, a wing rather than a part of the main structure, with living quarters for the sheriff's family and three small cells behind.

Dale Thorne opened the door and stepped into the bare, dusty room with its roll-top desk and three straight chairs. There was no one in the office so he knocked on the door to the adjoining living quarters.

A voice called, "Come in," and he pushed open the panel. Ben Underwood sat in an armchair, his slippered feet out before him, his steel-rimmed spectacles well down on his fleshy nose.

"Bronco!" The sheriff climbed to his feet and extended one thick palm. "Now this is a surprise."

"Hi, Uncle Ben." A full generation of youngsters had called this man Uncle Ben, for Sheriff Underwood was almost as permanent in the country as was Thunderhead, having held office for nearly thirty years. "I just rode in."

"Let me look at you." Ben Underwood had an old man's insistence. His voice was a little high, a little twangy as he spoke more through his nose than through his mouth. "I swear to Pete you look more like your dad every year." His tone changed. "Been to the ranch yet?"

"That's one of the things I want to talk to you about. I was there this morning. Les was killed last night."

The old man started. "Killed? How?"

"Shot in the back of the head, close up. Old Coke found him in the trail around midnight."

The sheriff tugged at his long lower lip thoughtfully. "Funny King didn't send a rider to tell me."

"You know King. He runs his own business."

"And I saw Ford at the saloon this afternoon. He didn't say anything."

"I don't think Ford knows it yet."

The sheriff spat into the cuspidor beside the chair. "Never could make King out. He's well named, I guess. Figures he's king of the whole place. Does mighty near like he pleases. Who does he think killed Les?"

"Maybe me. He wanted to know where I was last night."

"Where were you?"

"Back in the hills maybe twenty miles. I cut down through Squaw Canyon on the old logging road. You don't think I shot Les, do you?"

The old man shook his head. "King will come riding in here hell for leather sometime next week and expect me to dig up the killer without even having seen the body." He sighed. "Someday I'm going to quit this job. What do you intend to do now, boy?"

"That's another thing I came to see you about. I ran into Gus DuBois out in California. He claimed that Dad didn't leave the ranch to Ma, that he made a will the day before he died, that he left the ranch to me."

The sheriff lifted his spectacles and looked

26

intently at Dale. "That would make a slight difference."

Dale Thorne said, "One hell of a difference. I always knew that King married my mother to get the ranch, and I'm certain she married him because he was foreman, because she felt that a place as big as Thunderhead needed a strong man's hand."

"King's that all right."

"Such a will would mean that Thunderhead is mine, has always been mine, that it was mine before my mother married King, before either Les or Ford were born."

"Where is this will?"

Dale Thorne walked to the window and stared out at the now dark street, then swung back. "I don't know. DuBois didn't know. He said you witnessed it. He said you were the executor, that you had it in your safe."

The sheriff met his eyes squarely for a long minute, then let his own fall away. "If he said that he lied." The old voice was low, restrained. "I know nothing about it, Dale."

"But why should a dying man bother to lie to me?"

The sheriff took a long time to answer. "Gus DuBois was a strange man. He lived in this country for twenty years, and he never became a part of it. He was a gambler without nerve, a lawyer without principals, and he hated King

27

Parson as no man has ever hated another. Does that answer your question, Son?"

Dale Thorne stared back at him. In all the sorry years he had never felt so alone as he felt at this particular moment.

"Uncle Ben." He said it slowly. "Don't make me believe that you stayed in office all this time by making your peace with King."

Ben Underwood's leathery face reddened with rage and his thick brows drew down over narrowed, suddenly ugly eyes. "If I were twenty years younger I'd take you into the alley and whale the daylights out of you. Now, get out of here before I throw you in jail."

Thorne turned and walked to the door. "I believe DuBois." His voice was flat, final. "I'll be back, Uncle Ben. I didn't ride a thousand miles to lose Thunderhead again."

CHAPTER THREE

There were only two saloons worthy of the name in Climax, although on the side streets a half dozen hole-in-the-wall affairs catered to the small ranchers, the unattached riders and the drifters who wandered down from the hills.

The Palace was by far the more elaborate of the two, boasting a fancy backbar, hauled up by wagon all the way from Denver, the crystal chandelier which was Curt Walder's pride, and six poker tables where a good half of Climax's leading citizens usually congregated.

Ford Parson sat at a rear table, his back against the wall, his low-crowned black hat slanted back on his handsome head, his shirt clean and ruffled, and the tails of his dark broadcloth coat just touching the floor. He had a thin, tight face, his complexion was pale and there was a cold opaqueness to his blue eyes.

Watching him Dale Thorne thought that his brother consciously attempted to make himself look as much like a gambler as possible. Ford was just twenty-one, a year younger than Les, three years younger than Dale, but already there was a set about his thin-lipped mouth more to be expected in a man twice his years.

He was intent on the game and did not lift his

eyes when Dale moved up to watch the play.

He saw Ford lose two pots, then rake in a big one on three queens before he said,

"Speak to you for a moment?"

Parson turned his head and raised his eyes to his half-brother. "Well, I'll be damned! When did you find your way back?" There was no welcome in his too handsome face, no real feeling, only a mild surprise.

"Rode in this afternoon."

"Been to the ranch?"

Dale nodded.

Ford hesitated. It was obvious that he hated to leave the game. "Cash me in." He shoved the chips toward the house man, pushed back his chair and rose.

There were less than two dozen men in the saloon. Most of them had spoken to Dale when he first came in. Now they watched surreptitiously as the brothers moved to the far end of the bar.

The bartender brought a bottle of whiskey and two glasses. "Glad to see you back, Dale."

Thorne nodded and the man moved away. Ford Parson poured the drinks. Dale stood silent, trying to analyze their relationship.

He was the older brother and in the normal course of events Les and Ford might have followed him. But King Parson had always made it plain to his sons that they were Parsons and, therefore, of a superior breed, and should look down upon Dale because of his Thorne blood.

"King glad to see you?"

"Apparently you haven't heard."

Ford Parson raised his glass and drained it at a gulp. "Heard what?"

"Les was killed last night. Shot in the back of the head. Old Coke found him in the middle of the road."

Ford Parson looked at his brother sharply for an instant as if he did not believe it. Then he said slowly, "It's a wonder Coke could see him. When Coke left town last night he was loaded."

"Is that all you can say?"

Ford shrugged angrily, his mouth hard. "What am I supposed to do, cry? You've been gone three years. You don't know how things are. Les began to throw his weight around almost as soon as you left. He's been trying to tell me what to do. We had a hell of a fight two weeks ago and I whaled him. He said he'd shoot me if I ever came back to the ranch."

"Did you shoot him?"

Ford laughed suddenly, his teeth flashing white in the darkness of his face. "If I had, would you expect me to admit it?"

Dale shook his head.

"Matter of fact I didn't. I never left this room from six o'clock until four this morning. I won nearly a thousand dollars and some twenty people saw me do it. Did you?"

Dale said, "Why should I want to shoot Les?"

Ford's smile turned mocking. "Don't give me that brother business. You always hated us. You never forgave my father for marrying Ma, did you?"

Thorne didn't answer and, after pouring himself another drink Ford said, "Don't worry. I know you didn't shoot Les. But I've got a damn good idea who did."

"Who?"

"That I'm not going to tell you for several reasons. First, you might go after him, and that doesn't suit my purpose at the moment. Second, I can use the knowledge for some business of my own."

Dale Thorne studied his brother thoughtfully, and what he saw he did not like. In Ford he sensed the same animal ruthlessness which had driven King Parson to the top, plus an added calculating coldness never noticed in the older man.

King was utterly self-centered. What he wanted he took, yet he did so not by dissemblance but rather in a headlong rush which swept all opposition from his path.

"You have less feeling than anyone I've ever met."

Ford Parson laughed again, and put a hand on his brother's arm. "What are you talking about? Never since I can remember was there any love at Thunderhead. King cowed Ma. She was afraid to open her mouth when he was in the room, and he drove us kids—you because he didn't like you or your father before you, me and Les because we were Parsons and had to measure up to what he thought a man ought to be. But he doesn't love us, never did. He's never loved anything except himself and the ranch."

Thorne did not speak.

"Don't talk to me about love." There was something fierce in Ford Parson's tone. "Ma was the only one of the whole crowd who loved me, and she was too weak to respect. I don't hate you, my dear brother, but I despise you for being a sentimental fool. You love this country. You love Thunderhead. You always have. Me, I hate the ranch, the hard work, the blizzards, the constant tyranny with which King runs it and tried to run me."

His eyes became mocking. "Don't get any false ideas. When the time comes I'll demand every penny of my full share, but until King dies I want to stay as far away from it as possible."

Ford set his glass on the bar. His eyes challenged his brother for an instant, daring him to protest, then he turned deliberately away and started back toward the card game.

He stopped almost immediately. The saloon's flat door had been forced open. A horse's head appeared in the opening, then the animal clomped into the room, a girl upon its back.

She was slight, with fair wavy hair tucked up into a flat-crowned hat. She wore a man's shirt, the sleeves rolled up to expose her young forearms. Her nose was a trifle turned up, her mouth at the moment a hard, rigid line. Her blue eyes were angry yet chill.

"Lucy Colton." Dale Thorne said it half under his breath, and no one heard it for every eye in the room was on the girl. They hardly noticed the four men who strode into the room behind her, two fanning out to the left, two to the right.

"You!" She jerked her head at Ford Parson. "I warned you last week not to play cards with Vince again. Apparently you didn't believe me."

No one had noticed the coiled whip carried in her left hand, concealed partly by the horse which she had pulled around until he stood quartered toward Ford.

She shook it out now—a bull whip, short-handled with a long, buckskin lash beaded at the tip with tiny iron rings.

A wordless protest broke from Ford Parson's lips and unconsciously his right hand dropped to his gun.

The lash whistled out, darting like a striking snake, wrapping around his wrist. She gave a sharp yank and the now half-drawn gun spun clear across the width of the room to slam noisily against the far wall.

34

"You devil!" Ford was staring at his bleeding wrist.

The whip cracked as she brought it back and lashed at him again, this time aiming for his face.

He threw up both arms, ducking his head, and the steel cut through his coat and brought blood at the shoulder. The third stroke sent the lash whistling around his neck and, with a quick flip of her wrist, she dragged him from his feet, to fall on his knees, yelling as he went down.

The startling suddenness of Lucy Colton's attack on Ford took Dale by surprise. However, as she flailed again at Ford, who cowered on the dirty floor, trying to hunch himself against the punishment like a turtle retreating into its shell, Dale made a reckless move to interfere.

The girl was bringing the whip back over her head when he started forward. As the lash struck his brother's shoulders and curled about them, Dale lunged wildly at her.

She saw Dale's charging shape close upon her and attempted to retrieve the lash, but one of the metal bands caught in Ford's coat and for an instant the rawhide was a taut line over which Dale Thorne's fingers closed. He tugged heavily, throwing himself sidewise for more leverage, and jerked the hard handle from her grasp. It came across the gap as if the thong were elastic, and struck him on the side of his head.

But the blow was neither as sharp nor as heavy

as he caught an instant later, for one of the men who had followed Lucy Colton into the room jumped forward and brought the heavy barrel of his gun down on Dale Thorne's scalp.

Two things saved Thorne from having his skull crushed. One, the high-crowned hat he wore absorbed part of the blow. Second, the blow was not well centered. The gun barrel slipped along the side of his head, crashing down onto his shoulder. Still, it was enough to knock him flat for the instant.

He lay on his stomach, trying to steady his swaying senses. He stayed there for what seemed to him an age, then, when he started to get up he used a trick he had seen in California. He came up to his knees, shaking his head as if he did not know where he was. Then slowly he dragged himself upright, twisting so that when he came erect he was not facing the man who had struck him down, but quartered to him so that he only saw his face from the corner of his eye.

The man was big and thick-shouldered, larger even than King Parson. He was smiling a little now, his eyes wolfish and eager, his gun still held loosely in his hand. He watched his victim with obvious pleasure, then turned his head toward the girl.

In that second Dale Thorne moved. He twisted and leaped for the larger man, grabbing the wrist of the gun hand, wheeling around so that he got the forearm across the point of his hip, putting his full pressure on the wrist until the gun dropped. Then he spun away, swinging for the head as he turned.

The big man tried to duck, but Dale's crashing right took him high on the face and split the skin over the prominent cheekbone.

The man shook his head like an ox, and then lowering it charged his lighter opponent. Dale took two backward steps and, as the other came in, head still down, he brought up his left knee hard against the bullet chin. Then he chopped down with both hands, fingers laced, the calloused sides striking the bull-like neck in a savage rabbit punch.

The big man sank to his knees. He stayed there for what seemed a long time as Dale sucked air into his laboring lungs. Then he came up, apparently indestructible, and charged again, both huge arms swinging.

Dale clipped him on the chin, plunged a savage right under the heart, but for all the effect his blows had he might have been beating his fists against a stone wall. A fist caught his shoulder, spinning him half around. Another bounced off his ear, a third cut his upper lip.

He backed away, blood salty in his mouth, and saw the man leering at him, confident as he bored in again.

Dale side-stepped and buried his left in the

man's stomach, hearing the *whoosh* as air drove from the thick lips. There seemed no point in battering the hard head, so he put another right under the heart, a left hook to the stomach, and took a clubbing blow along the side of his head in return which made him stagger back against the bar. The brute lowered his head, rushed forward, and Dale weaved aside. Unable to halt his charge the man smashed heavily into the bar.

He seemed to hang there for an instant, completely immobile, and Dale hit him in that second, squarely on the back of the broad neck.

The man dropped. His head struck the foot rail with a popping sound. He did not move.

Dale leaned against the bar. His lungs ached with the effort of breathing. His ribs were sore from the pounding he had taken, and his lips and cheek were so swollen that his head felt lopsided.

"You there!" He heard the girl's voice as if from a great distance, but the words cut through the haze shrouding his mind.

He turned a little to look at Lucy Colton, still in her saddle, and stared grimly at the small pearl-handled gun she held in her gloved hand.

"Come over here!"

Dale's battered lips twisted. His impulse was to tell her to go to the devil. He came away from the bar, using his hands to shove his aching body upright.

Ford Parson stirred and sat up, his fine clothes stained with blood and refuse from the floor. Dale paid no attention. He moved directly to the girl and stared up at her.

She watched him, her blue eyes steady and coldly alert. "You're Dale Thorne, aren't you? I didn't recognize you at first."

He thought that he would have known her anywhere. She had changed less in three years than he would have expected. Then she had been a girl of eighteen, more leggy perhaps, a little less developed, but her face was the same.

There was an elfin quality about it in repose, but it was not in repose now. It was set in hard, stern angles, revealing the difficulty she was experiencing in restraining the anger that pulsed through her.

"Another Thunderhead hand to be dealt with."

He did not understand. Ford had picked himself off the floor, and now glared sullenly at the mounted girl and at the men who surrounded them.

One of the girl's crew had gone to examine the big fighter whom Dale had knocked down. He straightened at a question from Lucy Colton and said,

"He's coming around. You can't kill Sarcoff by hitting him on the head."

"Throw some water on him." There was no feeling in the chipped words.

39

The man looked at the bartender. The bartender nodded and lifted a half-filled pail from behind the counter. Deliberately the Colton rider threw it into his fellow's face.

The giant grunted. He sat up, cursing in a language which Dale did not understand. He was helped to his feet and stood, looking something like a great bear as he glowered at Dale.

The girl's voice was sharp, crisp. "Pick up your gun and get out."

Sarcoff stooped and swept his gun from the floor. His narrowed, hate-filled eyes were riveted on Dale as if he were tempted to shoot. Finally, he shrugged his thickly muscled shoulders, dropped the weapon into his holster, turned and shambled through the doorway.

Dale let out his breath slowly. He had not even been conscious that he was holding it.

The girl spoke to her men. "Take these two out, put them on horses and take them to the ranch."

Dale gaped at her, hardly believing his ears. "Now wait a minute. You can't do that."

"Can't I?" Her white teeth showed in a mirthless smile, and her eyes were as cold and steady as any he had ever seen. "You've got things to learn, Mr. Thorne. The day when Thunderhead ran this country is passing. There's going to be a new deal. We'll see how King Parson likes it."

"And what do you intend to do with us?" Dale's voice was tense and edgy.

She considered him as she would an animal she was thinking of buying. "I haven't decided yet. Maybe I'll hang both of you. Maybe I'll just break your fingers so you can't handle a gun and that card sharp brother of yours can't deal any more crooked hands. I'll tell you when I make up my mind. Go ahead. Take them out."

CHAPTER FOUR

Thunderhead Valley was in reality two valleys, connected by the canyon of the Loud River which snaked through the upper valley and emptied into a half-mile long lake. Ages earlier some underground upheaval had thrust up a dike of rock to block the river's course, and had flooded that area to create the lake.

The water had cut through the dike, forcing a passage through a fold in the hills, and deepened it over the years into Loud Canyon.

Climax stood at the mouth of Loud Canyon where the river burst out into the lower valley and threaded through the meadows to join the distant Platte.

Years before, when Ike Colton and Dan Thorne had brought their mixed herd north over the Goodnight trail and then swung west, and worked their way again northward until they found the twin valleys, this had all been Indian land.

But in the thirty years since, the valleys had changed, Climax had sprung to life, smaller ranches had moved into the tributary valleys, while mining and timber had brought men into the higher hills.

Still the two ranches, Thunderhead and the

Colton place, continued to dominate the life, the business and the actions of the people who lived in that part of the territory.

At first it had been one huge ranch, named for the mountain under which the original buildings had been raised, and no one had ever told Dale exactly what had caused the split. But some five years before his birth Ike Colton had quarreled with his partner.

The story ran that they had split the herd into two parts and cut cards to see who would retain the original ranch site and who would go to the south valley and there build a new spread of his own.

Dan Thorne had won. He had kept Thunderhead while Ike had trailed his animals back down through the pass. Ike Colton had built his new headquarters where the valley upended in the rising mountains to the south, and called it by his initials, the IC ranch.

The bitterness which had caused the split had not healed with the division of the herd, nor was it assuaged when Dan Thorne was thrown from his horse and killed.

Dale remembered his mother's story of how the Coltons had chosen to raid the herds during the time the crew was at his father's funeral. He knew how King Parson had led the retaliatory strike in which three of the Colton riders had been shot.

After that the fighting had subsided, but the hard feelings between the two crews had not lessened, and there were constant charges of rustling from both sides.

Dale rode now at his brother's stirrup. His wrists were looped with a buckskin thong, tied to the horn of his saddle. Inside of him was a tight, hot core of anger, most of it directed against the girl who sat straight-backed and alert at the head of the small column.

Two men rode before them, leading their horses. Two rode behind, ready at any moment to cut off any attempt at escape.

Dale glanced sidewise at his brother. Ford rode so close that their stirrups clinked from time to time, but he seemed submerged in his own thoughts, his shoulders hunched, his hat pulled low.

Dale said, "What started this?"

Ford turned his head. The moon was partly hidden by a thin cloud and his features were indistinct. "What ever starts it with the Coltons? They've been hunting a fight ever since I can remember."

"Lucy said something about your playing cards with Vince."

"I didn't ask him to sit in the game. He came to the Palace last night and bought in. I was already at the table. What was I supposed to do, cash in and leave?"

"It might have been better for both of us if you had."

Ford's laugh was short and without humor. "It's not my fault if the chump doesn't know how to play cards. And it's not my business to ask where he got the thousand dollars from."

"So he lost a thousand to you."

"Not to me. There were six men at the table. Sure, I won a little better than a thousand, but others won and lost, too. I don't know how much of what I got was his, how much came from someone else. The money didn't have a Colton stamp on it."

"She seems to think you were to blame."

"She's a hellcat." Ford said this viciously. "Since her father died last year she's changed things all around. Ike was getting pretty old, and the fight had gone out of him. I'd begun to hope that peace had come to Thunderhead at last. And then, as soon as he died this girl started hiring gunmen. That Russian, Sarcoff, you fought, is a bad hombre. And the men riding under him are scum. If I was Lucy I'd be afraid I'd get my throat cut."

"What's she been doing?"

"Keeping Thunderhead out of the lower valley. We used to drive our beef through here to the railroad, remember. We didn't last year. She sent word to King that she'd given orders to her crew to scatter any herd that tried to come through.

King cursed, but he didn't try it. A herd you're shipping isn't one you want stampeded. You can run more tallow off a steer in a night than you can put on in three months. King drove up through Squaw Canyon, and he lost a good five hundred head before he reached the railroad at Comrock."

Thorne smiled under cover of the darkness and his opinion of Lucy Colton rose. Anyone who could make King Parson back down on anything had his admiration. King had never been backed down in Dale's memory.

He was silent then as they rode on through the night until the ranch buildings loomed ahead suddenly, and they turned in at the short lane which led back to the yard.

The Colton ranch was not built until after sawmills had been brought into the country, with the result that its buildings were of plank instead of squared logs like those of Thunderhead.

They rode straight to the porch of the main house and the girl stepped down. She turned and walked swiftly back to where Dale and Ford sat silently in their saddles, their wrists still fastened to the horns, and stood looking up at them thoughtfully. Then she spoke to Sarcoff.

"Take the gambler and lock him in the room behind the bunkhouse. Untie this one and let him come in. I want to talk to him."

The foreman grunted. "I'd better stick around. This little buckaroo seems to think he's tough."

"Never mind," she said. "I've got my gun and he hasn't got his, and if he tries anything he'll never get clear of the yard."

The man moved then, untying the thong which held Dale's arms. "Climb down, mister, and watch your manners. I'd like nothing better than a chance to take you apart."

Dale swung painfully out of the saddle. He watched as the riders led his half-brother away, then he faced the girl, now standing on the porch above him.

"I hope you know what you're doing."

"I do." Her voice was steady, unhurried, as if she had complete confidence in herself. "Come inside."

He followed her slowly, his rugged features bleak and hard-set. A lamp burned in the hall, another in the big living room. Never in his life had he set foot inside this house before. For that matter he had never been in the ranch yard.

Lucy motioned him to a chair and he sat down as she peeled off her gloves and tossed them onto the dark wood table. He watched her closely.

He had gone to school with her in Climax because it was the only school the valley boasted, but she had been three grades behind him, and the feud which separated their families had held them apart.

"So you're starting a range war," he said bluntly.

She continued to look at him solidly. "The war, as you call it, was started before either you or I were born. My father spent his full life trying to keep what was rightfully his, first from Dan Thorne and then from King Parson. Vince and I have no choice but to carry on. I'll tell you one thing though. Ike was content merely to try to protect his property. I'm not. I'm going to break you, and King Parson, and his two sons." Her voice rose as she finished and a tide of color rose up into her cheeks.

"One son."

She started. "What does that mean?"

"Les was killed last night. We don't know who did it, yet."

Her eyes narrowed unpleasantly. "Are you implying that we killed him?"

Dale Thorne shook his head. "I don't think so. Whoever killed Les got up close, and I can't imagine him letting any Colton riders near him as long as he had a gun. I'd guess that whoever put that bullet into the back of his head was someone he mistook for a friend."

Some of Lucy's resentment seemed to fade for an instant with the news, then she caught herself up. "Les gave us more trouble than his father, and if you think his death will make any difference you're vastly mistaken. We mean to hold this valley clear to Climax. We mean to shoot any Thunderhead rider who crosses our range.

You can take that word back to King Parson."

He said roughly, "I don't carry messages to King Parson. I like him no better than you do. For your information I came home with but one purpose in mind—to run him off Thunderhead."

Her face showed that she did not believe him. "Run King off Thunderhead? But why would you want to run him from his ranch?"

"Because it isn't his ranch. Thunderhead belongs to me. It has ever since my father died."

Lucy was astonished. "Where did you get that idea?"

She was the last person in the world he would have thought of confiding in. In one sense, however, they were on the same side of the fence, since they were both fighting King Parson. "Do you remember the lawyer, Gus DuBois?"

She nodded. "A slight, gray man, with a limp and a hacking cough."

"I found him in California and he told me that the day before my father was killed he drew up a new will, leaving the ranch to me, not to my mother."

Lucy's eyes focused on him and he could almost see her agile mind turn over. "Why would he do that?"

This was the part that Dale found hard to tell. He said hesitantly, "To hear DuBois tell it, Dad didn't trust King Parson. He—he felt that King and Mother were interested in each other."

She drew a quick breath, then asked, "And where is this will? What happened to it?"

"DuBois said that Sheriff Ben signed as witness, that the will was given to the sheriff to keep in his safe."

Lucy took a half circuit of the room, moving over to gaze out of the window, then came back to face him.

"Have you talked to Sheriff Ben?"

He nodded. "He said about what I expected. But King has kept him in office for years. I believe DuBois."

"Because you want to."

His tone matched hers. "Because he was dying. There was no reason why he should lie."

"Unless he hated King Parson. Unless he chose this way to cause trouble, to turn you against King."

Dale watched her. "You seem to be defending King."

She said sharply, "There isn't anything in this world I wouldn't do to drive King Parson out of this valley. But I'm not a fool."

"Meaning I am?"

"Meaning that claim of this kind needs some kind of backing, more than the word of a discredited lawyer. Did he also suggest that King had had your father killed?"

Dale shook his head. "Nothing to that. Old Coke was riding with Dad that day. They were chasing a bunch of strays. The horse put his foot in a hole and Dad was thrown. He was dead when Coke reached him."

"Why are you telling me this?"

He said quietly, "Because you and I are both interested in the same thing. You want to get rid of King Parson. I want the ranch that belongs to me."

Lucy's upper lip curled in a gesture of contempt. "And you actually thought that I would throw in with anyone from Thunderhead? You're crazy. I've hated all of you people for too many years."

"That doesn't make sense," Dale protested.

"Why doesn't it? Listen to me. From the time I could first understand I've heard my father talk. Your dad got the home ranch. Your dad kept the best of the herd. And for years, before the railroad to the south went through, we had to get permission from your father to drive across his range to reach Squaw Valley.

"Now the boot is on the other foot. The railroad is much nearer on the south, so I stopped King last year. And I'll stop him this year and the next and the next. I don't need your help. I can break him alone. When I break him there will be no one on Thunderhead because all the stock will be gone."

"How do you figure that?"

She laughed tightly. It was a wicked sound in

51

the silence of the room. "It's easy. Three years ago we had a bad winter. Thunderhead isn't as sheltered as we are, and it hasn't as much hay. King lost half of his breeding stock. Last fall on the drive through Squaw Canyon he lost another five hundred head. He'll lose the same or more this year. And the small ranchers up in the hills are helping, nibbling at the herd.

"King's in trouble for money. And he'll be in worse trouble before I finish. Don't worry about your ranch, Mr. Thorne, because by the time I get through with it there won't be any ranch."

She turned abruptly and walked back to the window. "Sarcoff!"

A voice answered her from the shadowed yard.

"Come get Thorne and lock him up. I'll tell you what to do with him in the morning."

CHAPTER FIVE

Seated in the small room behind the bunkhouse Dale Thorne regarded his half-brother. Dried blood from the whipping still marred Ford's face and neck.

There was no water, no place to wash, and he knew that his own face carried the marks of his fight. "We're in a nice spot." He said it idly, though anger still simmered in him. "If I didn't know better I'd think that girl is crazy."

"Who says she's not?" Ford snapped. "In the last year she's been raising pure hell around here. She's nearly stripped her range of beef to get money, and she's spent it all hiring riders. You never saw a tougher crew in your life. I don't know what King said to her after Ike's death, but he probably got pretty rough, trying to scare her the way he's scared people all his life. This gal didn't scare." He touched the cuts on his neck with the tips of his fingers. "Damned if I don't admire her. She's got spunk even if she hasn't any sense."

"Funny her brother would play cards with you, his sister feeling the way she does," Dale said.

Ford's eyes opened wider. "Vince? He's all right. He's a cocky kid of course, but he doesn't have any feeling against Thunderhead and he knows I don't get along with King any better than he does with his sister." He fell silent, staring at his hands. The fingers were long, tapered, like a musician's or a surgeon's. "I wonder if she would actually do it?"

"What?"

"Break my fingers so I couldn't deal properly."

Thorne shrugged. "That's a bluff."

"No," Ford shook his head. "If you think that way you haven't read her right, my dear brother." His tone was mocking, almost amused. "That girl has put all softness behind her. She would order that Russian bully of hers to break my hand as simply as she would order him to kill a snake."

There was no fear in Ford Parson's voice, although Dale realized that he had already accepted the fact that he could be either mutilated or killed on this ranch.

But then, neither Ford nor Les had ever shown any kind of fear. They had amazed him as children, seeming insensible to the emotions which had wracked him.

Ford sensed what he was thinking about. It was a trick Ford had always had, the uncanny ability to read other people's minds.

"Come on, let's go to sleep. No matter what happens it will be easier with a good night's rest." He stood up. He started to unfasten his belt. "I could use a drink."

Dale felt that he could use one too. He bent

over to pull off his boots, and then he heard the sound at the rear door as the chain outside was loosened.

He straightened. The door eased open a couple of inches and a hushed voice outside whispered, "Blow out that lamp."

Ford Parson was across the room in a single leap. He blew out the light, plunging them into heavy darkness. "What is it, Vince?"

Dale had not recognized the voice. He realized now that it must be Vince Colton.

"I'm getting you out of here." The words were high-pitched and intense, as if the unseen man were laboring under the stress of great excitement or anger, or both.

"My sister hasn't got a brain in her head. What does she mean, riding into Climax that way just because I lost a few measly dollars at poker? What will the town think of me?"

Neither of the brothers answered him.

"There are two horses saddled, back in the edge of the timber. Get moving."

They shifted past Vince Colton into the semi-darkness of the yard, moving cautiously across the hard-packed ground toward the darker shadow which the trees cast on the rising hillside.

There was no light in the bunkhouse, but one lamp still burned in an upper room of the main house, and Dale Thorne half expected to be challenged before they reached the horses.

For awhile their moving figures were exposed in the openness of the yard, yet nothing happened, they found the mounts, lifted themselves into the saddles and swung toward the slowly rising back country.

They rode cautiously, single file, through the thick stand of trees, climbing until they reached a small cross canyon. They dropped down its easy slope and turned, thus coming back into the main Climax trail some three miles above the Colton ranch. At this point Dale swung his horse up beside his brother's, saying, "Lucky for us that Vince is decent."

"Decent?" Ford Parson sounded amused. "He's a young fool who can't wait to grow up to play the big man. The only reason he turned us loose was because he was afraid the valley would say that he had to hide behind his sister's skirts."

It ran through Dale's mind that everyone in the valley appeared to be at odds with everyone else, that the overall feud between the two ranches was nearly submerged in the squabbling among the people of both sides.

Vince Colton did not see eye to eye with his sister, and certainly Ford was doing nothing to help King carry on his fight.

They reached Climax just as light began to streak the eastern sky, and the hostler at the livery stable stared at them, surprise in his sleep-ridden face.

"I thought the Colton girl carried you fellows off."

Ford grunted. "Where'd you hear that?"

"It's all over town. Ain't seen the place so worked up since the last Indian scare twenty years ago. Joe Blonk sent a rider out to tell King. I thought it was them coming when I heard you ride up."

Ford's reaction was one of complete boredom. "King probably rolled over and went back to sleep. He'd likely pay Lucy Colton a bounty for cutting our throats. Come on, Dale. I'm going to bed."

Silently they walked up the empty street, using the road rather than the slatted boardwalk for some of the planks were broken, making footing hazardous in the predawn dark.

They turned in at the hotel, surprised to find Clara Austin curled up asleep in one of the big cane-bottom chairs.

She stirred waking at the sound of their entrance, and opened her eyes. Her red hair was a little rumpled, her face flushed from the sleep, and in the warmth of the soft light of the single lobby lamp it seemed to Dale that he had never seen anyone so pretty.

She stood up quickly, catching her breath as she saw the marks of the whip on Ford's neck and noticed Dale's puffed cheek and broken lip.

"You . . . she let you go!"

Ford Parson was a person who hated people to make much fuss over him. "You might say that." He turned rudely toward the stairs and climbed them, and they heard his steps as he moved along the upper hall to his room at the rear.

Dale and the girl looked at each other, both wordless for the moment, then he spoke awkwardly. "It was nice of you to sit up, to be worried about us."

She said tonelessly, "I couldn't go to bed. I kept thinking about Les. I kept thinking that that woman was probably going to wipe you all out as she murdered Les."

Dale Thorne's smile was wry. "I don't think she killed Les, but it's still nice that you were worried. It's been a long time since anyone took the trouble to worry about me."

Clara didn't question Dale about Les's murderer. She laid one hand on his arm, looking up appealingly into his face. "Or me. I'm as bad off as you are, Dale. Worse. When Les died I had no one left, no one to think of, no one to take care of me."

He took both her hands then, and the touch of her fingers against his were warming. "Don't be troubled. It's all right. Believe me, I'll see that nothing happens to you."

"Will you?" He knew the voice before he turned to see King Parson standing spread-legged in the hotel doorway. The rancher came forward into the lobby, walking stiffly, as if bothered by his long ride.

"I come racing into town to rescue you, and I find you romancing a girl."

Dale flushed. He glanced at Clara and saw that her face was red, that her green eyes were wide on King, and found in her strange, flustered expression something that he did not understand.

"It's none of your business what I do," Dale declared.

"No," the older man's eyes were hard on him. "It's none of my business what you do. I hear that the Colton woman has you her prisoner and I ride twenty miles to help, and it's none of my business. Where's Ford?"

"Upstairs. Asleep I guess."

"He would be. He's as near useless as a man can be. Get along with you."

Dale stared at him. He had been dismissed in this curt fashion many times in the past, but he had been younger then, his mother had still been alive and he had had to recognize King Parson as the final authority.

"I said get along. I want to talk to Clara."

Dale looked at the girl. Her eyes were on the floor now, not on him, and she said in a subdued voice, "You'd better go, Dale."

"You want me to leave you with him? You're sure?"

She raised her eyes then and gave him a small smile. "Yes. It's all right."

He nodded, not understanding what was happening here, and slowly climbed the stairs. At the top he paused to look back. Neither of them had moved. It was as if they both waited for him to be out of earshot.

He went on down the hall and pushed open his door, which he had not bothered to lock. It was so bright outside now that there was no need to light a lamp. He pulled off one boot and then the other, dropping them noisily to the floor. Then he did something he had never done before.

In his sock feet he eased back into the hall and slipped quietly along it to the stair head, stopping short of the point where he might be seen from below.

He listened intently, driven by curiosity and by an urgent need to understand the meaning of Clara's actions. He heard the grumble of King Parson's voice and peered forward to see into the lobby.

King held the girl by the shoulders, forcing her to look up at him. "Stop playing games with me, Clara. I won't let anyone cut between us."

Her answer was too low for Dale Thorne to catch.

"You're a fool," King went on. "Dale hasn't got the ranch and he won't have it, or even a part of it until I die. You're young. You want money and pretty things. You won't get them from Dale."

"Let me go," Clara pleaded.

King released his grip. "And you won't get them from Ford. You tried him before you took up with Les. Ford is the king who takes, not gives. When you discovered that he had no idea of marrying you, you took up with his brother."

She murmured something again too low to reach the upper hall.

"I don't care why you took up with him. I told you I'd never let you marry him. I'll never let you marry anyone but me."

The girl had pulled back a step and was staring at King Parson as if either horrified or fascinated. "*You* killed him." There was sudden conviction in her voice. "You killed your own son because of me."

King's hand snaked out and pulled her toward him, and there was more tense feeling in his voice than Dale Thorne had ever heard there before. "That's something you probably will never know, but I'll tell you this. I'd kill anyone who came between us. And I'll kill you before I let you go to another man. Just remember that."

CHAPTER SIX

Dale Thorne returned silently to his hotel room, but found it impossible to sleep. Clara's guess that King Parson had actually murdered his own son jarred Dale as nothing else had ever done.

Had King really killed Les because of the girl? The idea was fantastic, and yet the more he thought about it the more plausible it became. King had been younger than his mother, how much younger Dale could not remember, but he guessed that at the outside King was now not more than forty-five.

As for Clara, she had grown into a very attractive woman. Dale could understand how the thought of her could drive a man like King crazy.

He tried to picture what had happened on the murder night. Had King come in to see the girl? Had Les caught the two of them together? Had the men ridden out of town side by side, arguing, had King pushed his horse close to his son's and shot the boy in the head?

Dale got out of bed. With his mind churning like a cyclone it was ridiculous to try to sleep. From the window he saw that the sun was a good hour high in the eastern sky.

He dressed. He moved downstairs to the empty lobby. There was no sign of breakfast yet in the long dining room, but sounds came from the kitchen and he pushed open the door to see Clara bending over the big wood stove. Her face was pink with the heat and her red hair had pulled loose from its restraining knot to fall loosely around her slight shoulders. She heard him and turned.

"Dale."

He came in and shut the door. "I couldn't sleep. I did something awhile ago that I shouldn't have done. After I went upstairs and took off my boots I came back to the stair head. I listened to you talking with King."

Her eyes were very wide now. "You heard." It was hardly more than a whisper.

"I heard. Did King kill Les, Clara?"

She came away from the stove to face him across the width of the scrubbed kitchen table, and she took a long time to frame her answer.

"He didn't." She said it fiercely, as if she were trying to convince herself as much as him. "He couldn't have. No man would do a thing like that."

Dale's voice was tight in his throat. "I think maybe I know King better than you do. There's not a thing in this world King would not do if it turned to his advantage. How long has he been in love with you, Clara?"

The girl shook her head dazedly, but did not answer.

"Was King here on the night Les was killed?"

Still she didn't speak, and he reached across the table and grasped both her arms firmly. "Answer me."

"Dale, you're hurting me."

"I mean to hurt you." He stepped around the corner of the table without releasing his grip and drew her to him until their bodies touched. "I came back here a kid—an angry kid—who wanted something that belonged to him, but who still was not tough enough to get it. Ford told me. Ford said he didn't dislike me but he didn't respect me because I was too soft. Well, I'm back two days now and I'm telling you I've changed. I'm hard enough to fight King, or Ford, or the Coltons or anyone. Do you understand?"

She stared up at him, fear clouding her eyes.

"Answer my question. Was King Parson here to see you on the night Les was killed?"

She nodded, dumbly.

"Did Les know it? Did Les know that King was bothering you?"

"I never told him."

"But he could have known?"

She nodded again. "Oh, Dale, what am I going to do?"

He bent then, and kissed her. He had intended to. It was something outside himself, some power which seemed to be greater than himself which prompted the act.

Surprisingly her arms slipped around his neck and she returned his kiss, clinging to him, crying at the same time.

"How long has King been bothering you?"

"Six months, maybe."

"Has he said anything about marriage before last night?" He released her, but he did not step away and her hands remained on his shoulders.

She nodded again. "King isn't like other men. He—he started dropping by the hotel to eat. I didn't think anything about it. I'd been going to dances with Les, and I treated King as if he were already my father-in-law. Then one day last month we were alone in the lobby and he said that I was a fool, that Les was nothing but a wild kid, that what I needed was a real man. I misunderstood at first. I thought he was trying to tell me he didn't want me to marry into the family. I said that Les was of age, and should be able to marry without his father's consent. King laughed and said he didn't give a damn who Les married as long as it wasn't me—because he meant to marry me himself."

"What did he say this morning, after I first went upstairs?"

"He warned me to keep away from you. He said he meant to run you out of the valley."

"He'll work a long time to do that."

"Dale, I'm scared of King. Sometimes when he

looks at me I think he's crazy. And I'm afraid of myself."

"What do you mean by that?"

She said, "I want things. I want to get away from here and see something of the world. I'm tired of being poor."

"Meaning that you might marry King after all, even after he killed Les?"

"We don't know that he did. I said it, yes, but I haven't any proof and it's hard to believe that any man would do such a thing."

"You'd better believe it of King Parson." He said this grimly. "Let's stop talking about it for now. We'll have plenty of time. I mean to be around this valley for a long spell. What about some coffee?"

Clara nodded and turned to the stove, regaining some of her lost composure in the routine task. "Wouldn't you like some breakfast?"

"Bring it on."

They ate together at the kitchen table and as they sat there Dale watched her, a thought suddenly entered his mind. It was too soon to voice it, too soon after Les's death, but why shouldn't he marry her himself?

She had definite appeal. They had known each other for a long time and he had never before even seen a girl he wanted to marry, or for that matter thought of marriage with any seriousness.

Besides, the fact that King wanted her added

to his interest. His hatred of his stepfather had always been deep-seated, but now it was a burning thing, like a brand thrust against his side, eating into his flesh.

Now he not only wanted to recapture his ranch; he wanted to crush the man who had taken it from him; crush him utterly as he had watched King slowly crush his mother.

He rose, finding tobacco and building a cigarette. "Which is Ford's room?"

"The one on the left of the hall at the rear. But he won't be awake for hours."

"Want to bet?" He grinned at her and, bending over, planted a small kiss behind her ear. "Listen, honey, you stop worrying about King. Understand? You let Dale do the worrying from now on."

He was conscious as he left the kitchen that she watched him and that there was speculation in her gray-green eyes.

At the top of the stairs he walked unhesitatingly to his brother's room. The door was not locked. He could not recall ever having seen a door locked in Climax, and he wondered why the hotel bothered with the pretense of keys.

He pushed the door open to see Ford stretched out on his back, his mouth half open, snoring happily.

He walked over and shook the bed.

Ford waked at once. His eyes came open and

he lay perfectly still, looking owlishly up at Dale.

"What the hell?"

"I want to talk to you."

Ford shut his eyes. He groaned. "Why in the devil does anyone ever want to talk before noon? Go away."

Dale shook him again. "Listen to me. This is important. I think your father killed Les."

Ford's eyes popped back open. He sighed heavily and swung his feet out of the bed, sitting on its edge in his underclothes, running his hands through his thick black hair as if he thought that by so doing he could clear the lingering traces of sleep from his bemused mind.

He had apparently dropped into bed without bothering to wash, for the shoulder of the union suit still showed the cut where Lucy Colton's whip had split it, and dried blood made a brown stain around the hole.

"Where did you get that bright idea?"

Dale told him of what he had overheard, of talking to the girl in the kitchen. He left out a mention that he had kissed her.

Ford yawned. "It's possible. King's been smelling around that hive for months. There's no love-sick fool like an old one, but hell, I didn't think he figured to marry her. I guess she just won't play any other way."

Dale throttled an impulse to hit him. Ford was so utterly cold-blooded where human emotions were concerned. Apparently it did not trouble him in the least that his own father might have murdered his brother over a woman.

He said tightly, "King isn't going to marry her."

Ford stood up. "You're damn right he's not. If she married him the only reason would be to grab off a piece of the ranch, and I'm not going to let any little floozy get away with that."

"It isn't her fault that King's annoying her. You've got no call to name her that."

Ford had moved to the wash basin and was splashing water on his head. He looked up, his face dripping. "Grow up, kid. I've said before that you're soft and there's not much point in repeating myself, but don't be more of a sap than you have to be. Has she started to make a play for you already?"

"Now what are you talking about?"

Ford dried his face and hung the towel on a peg. "I know the signs. Clara's a good looking hen, and she's got a wicked pair of eyes, and she's fed up with running this hotel. She even made a few moves in my direction before she found out it didn't buy her anything. Then she lit on Les, and no matter what she told you she hasn't exactly discouraged King."

"I don't believe it."

"Believe what you like. Sleep with her, marry her, do whatever you choose. I don't care, but I'll not sit by and watch her grab off King. The way

69

she acts she'd get every dollar he ever saw out of him in a month."

Dale started to answer, then shrugged and walked out of the room, slamming the door. Behind its shaking panel he heard Ford's laugh, a nasty sound, without humor or pleasure.

Dale was burning inside, reflecting angrily that Ford dirtied everything he spoke about. Quickly he descended the stairs and stepped out onto the gallery. The morning air was clear and sharp and sweet and the mountains, surrounding the valley like a tree-studded fence, stood out in vivid relief against the crystal sky.

He sat down in one of the gallery chairs and propped his boots on the low rail. He was still sitting there when a rider ambled along the sidewalk, moving aimlessly until he stopped in front of Thorne.

"Are you Dale Thorne?"

Thorne looked down at him, trying to recall the face. It was rather narrow, with high cheekbones which might indicate a trace of Indian blood in his heritage. As far as he could remember he had never seen the man before.

"That's right."

"My name's Arthur. I got a message from Old Coke."

Thorne had been leaning back against the wall in his chair. He straightened. "What's Coke want?"

"He's found out something about Les's death. He wants you to meet him at the line camp in Storm Canyon. He was afraid to try to come to town. King's watching him."

"What's he found?"

Arthur shrugged his narrow shoulders. "Beats me. Coke don't talk too much, and I'm taking a chance doing this, but Coke pulled me out from under a horse last year and I owe him the favor."

"How's the best way to get to the camp from here? I don't remember it."

"New last year. Get your horse. I'll show you."

He waited until Thorne came down the steps and they walked side by side toward the Livery.

"Been on Thunderhead long?"

The man Arthur shrugged. " 'Bout a year. Don't like it much. That Parson throws too long a shadow to suit me. Think I'll drift out after roundup. Have a stake by then."

Thorne was satisfied. He thought it might be worthwhile to keep contact with Arthur. It was apparent that the man did not feel too much loyalty to his stepfather.

They left town, heading north through Loud Canyon, coming out beyond the hills on the rolling spread of the huge Thunderhead range. It gave Thorne a lift, just to know that he was once again riding across her grass.

They skirted the bench, climbing for about three miles, coming thus to the mouth of a draw canyon, turning into the faint trace which led up the little creek.

They had covered nearly a mile when Thorne saw the outline of a cabin and the small corral. There was a horse in the corral, and he assumed it to be Coke's.

As they approached the camp he was surprised that the old man didn't appear, and turned questioningly toward Arthur.

"Sure he's here?"

The man nodded. "That's his horse. Go on in. I'll keep watch that no one rides up while you're talking."

A sixth sense tugged at Thorne's mind. It was something he could not quite identify, but there was the feel of danger around the place.

"Coke!" He made no move to step from the saddle, no move to get closer to the shack. "Coke, answer me."

He heard Arthur swear behind him, and turned to see the man swing his horse around and drive to the right. Thorne's own horse was in motion in the opposite direction before the first rifle cut loose from the brush. His gun was in his hand and he put a bullet squarely between the shoulder blades of the fleeing Arthur. Then, crouched low as an Indian, he spurred for the table of aspen and pole pine on the slope behind the cabin, bullets spattering around him.

How he made it he never afterward knew. One

bullet had clipped through the skirt of his coat, another peeled leather from his saddle horn, but it was seconds only before the timber closed around them and he put the driven horse at the canyon wall which steepened rapidly.

He rode upward perhaps a hundred feet and then was forced to turn. A rock face rose up out of the timber like an abutment to block his path.

Below him he could hear the crash of horses, the curses of his pursuers and angry shouts as someone hurled orders to cut him off.

It was not his stepfather's voice and he concluded that King was not in the ambushing party, but he never doubted that King Parson had planned this—had sent Arthur to toll him into a death trap.

Thorne's mouth was a grim line, his gun held ready in his hand. Actually, now that he had slipped through the jaws of the trap, he was not too worried.

In the timber, with his carefully trained horse, he felt certain that he could get away from anyone who came after him. And while he had not known where the line camp was, he did know this country and this ridge. He had hunted here as a boy, traveling every foot of the mountain shoulder which separated Thunderhead from the IC ranch on the other side.

The bushwhackers were gaining on him, angling up the slope, before he found a deer trail which ran toward the crest and put his horse into it. He wasted no time in shooting, knowing that his chances of hitting any of the men below was very slight.

Occasionally one of the tracking party fired, the bullet screaming through the trees or ricocheting from an outcrop of rock, but by the time he reached the broken crest the sounds of the chase had lessened. He started down the far side, easing the gait, feeling certain that once he reached the Colton range there was little danger of the Thunderhead crew following him further.

He dropped into a tiny canyon with a bubbling spring, stepped down to let his horse drink, then slaked his own thirst.

Afterward he rode on downward, no longer concerned with hiding the signs of his progress since he had eluded his pursuers. He wondered what Parson's next move would be, and tried to decide on his own.

He traveled through the sharp lip of the canyon and rode across a small meadow, stopping suddenly. There, plain in the soft earth, were the fresh tracks of half a dozen shod horses.

He looked around quickly, and was just in time to see a big man emerge from the brush, a rifle held ready, and to hear the guttural voice call, "Step down, Thorne. Welcome to the IC Ranch!"

CHAPTER SEVEN

Thorne sat frozen in his saddle. His first impulse was to spur his horse toward the trees, but the way the burly Russian held the rifle was more threat than any words. He'd never make it. And the chances were that Sarcoff would not shoot if he surrendered.

After all, the Colton crew did not have anything against him personally, and certainly they were not working for his stepfather.

Four other men appeared from the brush, advancing on him, guns drawn, in a loose half circle as if at any moment they expected him to try for his gun.

He didn't. He swung down, careful to keep his hands in sight, watching them stalk him hungrily.

"Look, I've got no fight with you."

"You are on our land." It was Sarcoff. "The orders are that no one from Thunderhead crosses that ridge."

"I'm not from Thunderhead. In fact, my stepfather just tried to have me killed, less than an hour ago."

"Take your gun slow, and drop it."

Thorne obeyed.

"Now step back."

75

He took six backward steps and watched one of the men scoop up his gun.

"All right," said Sarcoff, his craggy features marred by an ugly leer. "You think you lick me in the saloon, don't you? No one licks Sarcoff. No one." He unfastened his gun belt and handed it with his rifle to the man nearest him.

"If he tries to run, shoot him."

Dale Thorne looked at the huge figure. He guessed that Sarcoff weighed about two hundred and sixty pounds and none of it was fat. He stood at least six-feet-six, and his arms looked like the trunks of half-grown trees.

He was grinning, licking his thick lips as if he were seeing a tempting meal. The crew was also grinning. Obviously they waited with pleasure for the forthcoming fight.

There was no escape, no appeal from the slaughter planned for him. If he tried to run they would shoot him down. Desperately he girded himself for action, determined to hurt this solid giant of a man as much as possible. He had no real confidence that he could win, but at least he would deal out some punishment.

Removing his coat, he threw it aside. Then he unfastened his belt and let it drop. He wished that he were not in high-heeled boots. His only chance was to stay away from the giant as much as possible. Once Sarcoff's powerful arms locked around him he would be finished.

He watched the man stalk forward, but instead of waiting for the other's charge he suddenly leaped in, swinging a right with all the power of his running jump, plunging it into the stomach that protruded a little over the belt line.

He heard Sarcoff's agonized gasp for breath and knew that he had hurt him, and saw the big arms come around in a sweeping embrace and ducked under them, driving another blow to the stomach as he danced away.

Sarcoff stopped. He stared at Thorne, four feet away from him, his eyes muddy with pain. "Come on and fight."

"Come and get me."

The giant charged, but this time he had learned craft. As Thorne swung for the body he reached out with his huge hands and snared the lighter man's wrist, dragging him in close and wrapping his arms about him.

Thorne battled to free himself, driving short jabs against the barrel-like ribs, but it was a hopeless thing—like hitting a hogshead of nails. The arms tightened, increasing the pressure on his back until he thought his bones would crack.

There was a red haze before his eyes now and it turned steadily darker. If he did not breathe soon he would die.

Suddenly, inexplicably, the Russian released his grip. Thorne's legs were like rubber. He took half a step backward, gulping desperately for air.

77

He saw Sarcoff's face through a continuing haze, watching him in surprise, unable to lift his lead-weighted arms, wondering that the man showed this sign of human feeling.

And then he realized that this was not the case. Sarcoff had not loosened his hold from any pity. Deliberately he raised a big fist and drove it into the nearly helpless Thorne's face, slamming him backward, mashing the cartilage across his nose.

He swaggered forward and stood over Thorne, his grin wolfish.

"Get up and fight."

Thorne made no effort to rise. Even had he wanted to he doubted that he could make it, and he definitely did not want to. Only a fool would go up against this human block, only a man driven by desperation could even hope to stand up with Sarcoff.

"Get him on his feet. I'll teach him to battle Max Sarcoff."

Two of the riders leaped forward and caught Thorne by the arms, hauling him upright. The big man stood in close and shot his fist into Thorne's mouth, against his cheek, into his eyes. The blows were short, studied, deliberate, cutting rather than crushing, as if their purpose was to inflict pain rather than to knock him out. But the last blow to the chin was too hard, and Thorne slumped between the supporting riders.

Sarcoff stood spread-legged, staring down at him as if in surprise. "Can't take it, huh? Bring him to."

They brought him to by carrying him to the small creek and dumping him into a round pond. Then they yanked him out, sputtering and groggy, and marched him back to where the big man waited.

Sarcoff examined him, grimacing, showing his yellow teeth like a mangy bear.

"So he decided to wake up."

"You'll kill him, Max." It was one of the riders who held his arms. Thorne could not see him; he could barely see anything through his swelling eyes.

"All right, boys, you saw him with that calf. We've got to show these Thunderhead rustlers that the boss meant what she said when she warned them to keep off our grass or get hanged. Fetch a rope."

Dale Thorne shook his head, trying to clear it. His neck felt broken. Every part of his body ached with a stinging throb as if he had been seared by the hot flames of a fire, but his mind was slowly beginning to function again, and he could not believe what he heard.

"Hang me?" It was a croak. Why should these men want to hang him? He had done nothing except fight with Sarcoff. "You're joking."

"He thinks we're joking." Sarcoff's bull-like

laugh roared out across the meadow. His eyes were evil slits in his face. "He thinks we're joking. It's a joke all right. Hang him, and then we'll cut him down and snake him across the ridge and leave what's left at Thunderhead line camp. Bring up his horse."

Dale Thorne had known that all men die, and in his three years of wandering he had witnessed violence in a dozen places, but he had not expected to die here. It was ironical, he realized as he saw them leading up his horse, that he should have escaped his stepfather's men only to ride into this brutal group.

Strangely enough, he did not much care what happened to him. Awareness had been mostly beaten out of him. It was as if he had been given some drug which deadened his emotions, including fear, so that he was conscious of things around him in a detached way, without feeling that he himself had much part in the action.

The IC riders lifted him onto his horse. They tossed the loop around his neck and led him to a tree beside the creek.

Then he heard a woman's voice come out of nowhere, as from a dream. He turned his head, but his cheeks and eyelids were so bloated by Sarcoff's pounding that he could not see her.

"What's going on here?"

The man leading his horse stopped. The man riding beside him, holding him upright in the saddle, said something in an undertone which sounded like an oath.

Dale Thorne's heart leaped for a moment, then dropped. He knew the voice, Lucy Colton's, but he had no reason to expect mercy at her hands. He still remembered vividly how she had looked when she rode the horse into the bar, when she had whipped his brother, and when she had carried them captive back to the IC ranch.

Sarcoff said, "We caught him trying to brand a calf."

There was a long moment of silence. "Where's the calf?"

"It ran off into the brush."

"Where's the fire he was using?"

Another interval of silence. "Hell," said Sarcoff. "So there wasn't a calf. We caught him on IC range. You said to hang any Thunderhead rider we caught on our grass."

"You lied to me." Her voice bit like the stroke of her whip. "Why did you do that?"

The rider supporting him released his grip on Dale's arm. Thorne sagged from the saddle. He tried to catch the horn but failed. He knew he was falling, but he never knew when he hit the ground.

He regained consciousness in a bed, and had no idea where he was. A wet cloth lay over his swollen eyes and he swept it to one side, attempting to see. He could distinguish light but

81

little else. At least, he knew, he wasn't blind.

A hand came out to replace the cloth and Lucy's voice said, "Lie still. It's all right."

"Where am I?"

"At my ranch. You took a terrible beating, but you have no broken bones. The doctor was here. He said you would be all right, but it will take two weeks."

He lay perfectly quiet. "How long have I been here?"

"Since yesterday."

His voice was terribly tired. "I guess I wouldn't be here if you hadn't ridden up."

"I guess not. What did you do to Sarcoff to bring on this beating?"

"Nothing." Slowly, painfully, he told her what had happened, about the ambush his stepfather had set, about coming over the ridge and running into her men. "I was a fool." His voice now was hardly more than a whisper. "But I was so proud of myself for getting away from the Thunderhead crew that I blundered into Sarcoff. Another mistake like that will get me killed."

She listened, her face holding an expression of incredulity which he could not see.

"But why would King want to murder you?"

"For the same reason he killed Les. Because of Clara Austin."

"Do you believe King killed his own son?"

"King Parson would wipe out anything that

stands in his way. You think you know him? You have no idea what he is. You can't have unless you've lived with him. He's a sadistic throwback, a monster. I watched what he did to my mother, grinding her into her grave. I watched him drive his own sons until they hate the ground he walks on. I know what he did to me."

"But Clara—"

Dale's voice gained a little strength. "Of course he wants her, just as he wants anything of value— everything that is beautiful."

He could not see the look Lucy Colton gave him. "I think you'll find that Clara can take care of herself."

He stirred. "You don't know her. You haven't any idea."

He lay back then, exhausted, and suddenly he slept. He never knew that Lucy Colton came over to stand beside the bed, to stare down at his battered face.

A sob caught in her throat. "I should get rid of Sarcoff. I should drive him off the range like the beast he is. But I can't because I need him—and I need the bush riders who follow him." She turned away, her eyes haunted. "Where will it end?" She asked herself in sudden dread. One thing she did know, however, was that as long as King Parson rode the valley she had to be there to stop him, to protect Vince's interest.

CHAPTER EIGHT

By morning of the third day Dale Thorne was on his feet. His eyes were still discolored, but at least he could see his reflection in the mirror, and what he saw shocked him.

His face was marked, cut in a dozen places, black and blue from the iron knuckles of the Russian's fists. He shaved, steadying himself with one hand on the wash stand. A noise at the door made him glance quickly in the mirror, expecting to see Lucy Colton. Instead, it was her brother.

Vince came curiously into the room. He was slight with a rather thin face and yellow hair, and a mocking mouth as if he laughed at the world.

Dale Thorne eased around, wiping his face, and Vince looked at him critically.

"You look terrible. Sarcoff really gave you a working over. If he'd done that to me I'd kill him."

"Maybe I will." Thorne's voice was guarded. He did not know quite how to take this younger brother of Lucy Colton. He had never known him. Vince had still been in grammar school when he stopped going to Climax for education, and their family differences would have kept them apart at any rate.

"I haven't thanked you for turning Ford and me loose the other night."

Vince glanced over his shoulder to make certain that the hall behind him was clear. When he answered it was in a lower tone.

"Don't talk so loud. Lucy hasn't figured out yet how you got free. If she ever does she'll skin me alive."

Dale reached for his shirt, which had been washed and carefully ironed. "Maybe she's changed her mind in the last couple of days."

"Who, Lucy?" The boy, for he was little more, laughed silently. "You don't know her, friend. Just because she picked up your carcass and brought you here and nursed you doesn't mean she's changed in the least."

"That's hard to believe. She saved my life."

"Sure, she's soft underneath, like all women." Vince spoke with the intemperance of youth. "But when the old man died she set herself to one job—ruining Thunderhead."

"King Parson, you mean."

Vince came on into the room and sat down on the side of the bed. "That's where you're wrong. It's the name Thunderhead that gets her. You'd have to have known my old man and the way he hated that ranch to understand. I hear you claim it belongs to you, that you want to take it away from King?"

"That's right."

"So if you do you'll still have Lucy to fight."

Thorne had turned and was again watching the boy in the mirror. "I judge that you don't share your sister's feelings?"

"I think she's stupid." Vince's voice was casual. "I agree with Ford. What in hell is all the shooting about? Just because my old man and yours hated each other, is that any reason for me to lie out in the brush with a rifle and take pot shots at you as you ride past?"

Dale Thorne could think of no answer.

"This country is for the birds anyhow. Me, I want to see the world. There are a lot of places outside this valley, and a lot of things to do aside from chasing cattle through thorny brush, cooking in summer and freezing to death in winter. By the way, you've been around, you've been to Texas and California. What was the biggest city you've ever been in?"

Dale thought about it for a moment. "San Francisco, I guess."

"Like it?"

He thought again. "Some ways yes, mostly no."

"Why?"

"I guess I'm just a ranch hand. The most I want out of this life is Thunderhead."

"You'll never get it. You had a sample of what our crew can do. They're tough. They get pleasure out of hurting people. It makes them feel important. Do you know that most of them are outlaws? Sarcoff's wanted in half a dozen states, and I admit I'm afraid of him. Give him four or five drinks and no one knows what he'll do."

Dale Thorne had his shirt fastened. "Too bad we can't throw him up against King. That should be a fight worth seeing."

"It'll come to that. But while you're talking don't forget Mark Jacoby. You don't know him. He came to Thunderhead after your time, but I saw him lick four men in the Palace one night, and throw them into the street one after another. Mister, you sure picked yourself a chore. You still think you want Thunderhead bad enough to fight for it?"

"I'm going to have it." Thorne said simply, without bragging.

"What are you going to do for a crew? It takes money to hire gunslingers. It's breaking this ranch, holding the crew Lucy's paying. Seems to me the only ones getting anything out of our fight are the gunhands."

"I haven't got that kind of money."

"It would take thirty men, and then you might get whipped."

"I'll find them."

Vince stood up. "I guess Ford's right. He and I are the only two smart ones in the whole territory."

Dale studied him curiously. He started to say, "If I were you I'd pick someone beside

Ford Parson as a model." Then he didn't. What business was it of his what this boy did?

He said, "Give me a hand, will you? This left leg doesn't seem to work like it should."

And so he walked out to the dining room of the IC ranch, leaning on Vince Colton's shoulder.

Lucy Colton came through the kitchen door carrying a tray. She stopped in surprise. "You shouldn't be up. I was bringing your breakfast."

He managed a grin with his battered lips. "I couldn't stay in bed until I put down roots. First time in my life I ever stayed down three days."

"You're in no shape to ride."

He knew that. The walk from the bedroom had taken his full reserve of strength, and he felt a little light-headed. But he stubbornly lowered himself into a chair at the table.

"No call for you to lug a tray in to me. I can still walk to food. Anyhow, I certainly never expected to see the day when the Coltons were feeding someone from Thunderhead."

She set the tray before him and stepped back, regarding him with a frown. "I don't quite know what to do with you."

He glanced at her quizzically without replying.

She spoke slowly, as if talking to herself. "I've always heard that a person should never save another's life, because ever afterward they feel responsible for the one they saved. You're something of a problem, Mr. Dale Thorne."

"How's that?"

"I don't want you riding out of here until you're fit to ride. But that doesn't mean I'll stop fighting you. I don't want you on Thunderhead any more than I want King there."

"At least that's plain enough."

"No," she said, her lovely cheeks set in hard, resolute planes. "It isn't plain enough. If I were as tough as I should be, as Sarcoff thinks I am, I'd have let them hang you the other day. What I'm trying to say is that as long as you are here you are safe, but as soon as you ride off the ranch all bets are off."

"That sounds fair."

"You don't understand." She was very earnest now. "Sarcoff hates you. I think it's because he butted the bar the other night in the saloon when you two were fighting, and knocked himself out. It hurt his pride, and he has a lot of pride. He regards himself as the toughest, strongest man in the world. And I've had to go along, to listen to his boasting to let him have a free hand in running the ranch.

"I have to feed his ego to make him stay here because I need him. Can you understand that? I've got a wild crew, and no one but a man like Sarcoff could hold them in line. I saw him take two riders yesterday, each by the back of the shirt, and bash their heads together. It knocked both of them cold."

He searched her words as he listened, hearing behind them a note of near despair. Lucy Colton was beginning to realize that she was no longer a free agent, that in building a machine to fight a range war she had, in turn, become a captive of that machine.

He looked around to see how Vince was taking it and was surprised to find that the boy had left the room.

He said slowly, "You're scared, aren't you?"

"Scared?" A trace of color flared in Lucy's face. "Scared of what?"

"Of Sarcoff. Of what you've set in motion."

She started to answer him hotly, then checked herself and said in a controlled voice, "Not scared, Bronco, not scared for myself, but scared for the people who stand up against me. Much as I hate Thunderhead and your family, I hate murder more, and I'm only beginning to realize that men wild enough to fight my battles are not controllable. This crew of mine actually enjoys killing, hurting, maiming. There was hardly a man with Sarcoff who did not get pleasure out of seeing you beaten, yet they had nothing against you personally. They did not share Sarcoff's feeling against you. They merely like to see blood."

Suddenly Dale felt sorry for her. It was an emotion he had never expected to entertain for Lucy Colton. She was so dominant, so self-possessed, but he saw her now as a slip of a girl, with her back to the wall, fighting King Parson whom no man had ever been able to whip, tormented by the knowledge that the crew she used might run wild at any time, like a pack of lobo wolves.

"Get rid of them," he said. "Get rid of them as you would a case of frozen dynamite that's turned unstable. You don't know when they will explode, and it will drive you insane thinking about it."

"Are you crazy? King Parson would raid me in a week."

"Look," he said, leaning forward in his intensity. "I owe you a lot, and I won't forget it. Meanwhile, you and I have no basic quarrel. What happened between our families happened a long time ago. Let me raise a crew, let us join forces and drive King off Thunderhead. I'm going to do it anyway. I'm going to do it if it is the last thing I do on this earth."

"Are you suggesting that we form a partnership?"

Dale shook his head. "Merely that we get together to clear the valley of all the riff-raff, of the gunslingers and killers. Then we'll run the ranches as they were, you and Vince with this, I with Thunderhead."

"What about Ford?" Lucy demanded, her mouth tight and hard.

He had forgotten Ford. If he proved that the ranch was his, always had been his, long before Ford was born, where did it leave his half-brother? Dale sighed.

"That is something I will have to work out."

"Ford won't like it that way. He'll be on the other side."

Yes, Ford would be on the other side. There was no question of that.

"And what do you intend to do for a crew, to replace the men you want me to fire? Who's going to help you take back Thunderhead?"

He said, "There are a lot of small ranchers in the hills, bush riders. They all hate King Parson. He's ridden over their places and cut their fences and accused them of rustling from him."

"Most of them did," Lucy pointed out.

"Sure, and in their place I'd have done the same thing. I used to ride those hills when I was a boy. I knew most of those people and I never had any trouble with them. I think most of them sympathized with me because they knew I didn't get along with King."

"That isn't much to justify a hope of getting them to help you now. King has a different crew than he used to have. They are in a class with my own men, and the hill people are afraid of them. I wouldn't count on raising a crew that way. If you do you are a bigger fool than I think you are. The answer is no. I'll play out my hand alone." She turned, once again in command of herself, and started for the kitchen. Suddenly she stopped.

"One thing more. Don't try to leave this house."

It was Dale's turn to stare. "You mean I'm a prisoner?"

"I mean that as long as you keep out of sight I don't think the men will bother you. If you go out they'll bait you into another fight." She disappeared through the doorway, leaving him alone with his thoughts. They were far from pleasant.

He stayed for two more days, then, although his hurts had not yet healed, he decided on riding for town.

It bothered him that the girl insisted that she and Vince accompany him. She had Vince bring the horses up to the steps of the main house, and they came out to find most of the crew grouped in a tight knot below the corral.

They made no move to interfere, but as he rode past there were catcalls and Sarcoff stepped forward.

"Thorne. You hear me."

He did not answer.

"Be out of the country as soon as you can. If I run into you again, you die. Understand?"

CHAPTER NINE

Clara Austin gasped at sight of Dale's face. He had come into the lobby weary from the long ride, to find her behind the desk.

"Dale, what happened to you?"

He told her, noting with warm pleasure the concern in her gray-green eyes. He told her about the ambush, about riding over the ridge and running into the Colton men.

"They damn near finished what King started. That should make him laugh."

She said, "I don't think King had anything to do with it."

"What makes you say that?"

"He was here last night. He was worried about you."

"This I'd have to see to believe."

"He was. We had a long talk. He was different, Dale. I think the shock of Les's death has changed him."

"The only thing that will ever change King is a bullet, and even when he's dead I doubt that the worms will work on him. He's too tough."

"What a horrible thing to say. I know how you feel, Dale." She laid a small hand over his large one where it rested upon the desk. "But I never saw King the way he was last night. If any of the Thunderhead crew attacked you it was Mark Jacoby's idea, not King's. Mark is a killer if I ever saw one. He gives me the creeps, just the way he looks at people. I think it was he who killed Les."

"So you've changed your mind about King doing it?"

Clara tightened the grip across the back of his bruised hand until he winced unconsciously. "I said that I talked to King last night, for nearly three hours. He was a different person. He showed me a gentle side that I'd never seen before."

The sarcasm in Dale's tone was strong. "It's a side few people have seen, believe me. He never showed it to my mother."

"He explained that, too." Clara was speaking rapidly, as though to convince herself even more than him. "He said that he never really loved your mother, that she was just a woman left alone with a small child and a big ranch. . . ."

"And he wanted the ranch," Dale stated grimly.

"I don't think you're quite fair."

He loosened his hand. "Clara, I believe you know what I think of you. Don't be taken in by King Parson. He can be agreeable when he wants to, even be charming."

"And he loves me."

Dale Thorne drew a long breath. "What would you say if I told you that I love you?"

Her eyes went very wide. "Why, Dale. You've hardly seen me in three years."

"What's time got to do with it?"

"I—I don't know." Her voice was unsteady and a strange, veiled look came into her eyes.

"You were going to marry Les. Did you love him?"

She said slowly, "I thought I did. I—I'm all mixed up, Dale. I'm trying to be very honest with you, and it isn't easy."

"Were you marrying Les only to get a part of the ranch? Is that why you're fooling around with King?" There was a barbed sting to his words.

"What a thing to say." Clara's face reddened in anger and her eyes darkened. "I certainly don't like you when you talk that way."

His voice was rough. "How do you want me to talk? I know that the things you're saying about King aren't true. I know what he is, yet you seem to be willing to kid yourself into believing them."

"I don't want to hear any more."

"All right. But listen to this. No matter what King Parson tells you, he will never give you Thunderhead. Because it belongs to me." He swung away and climbed the stairs, exhausted from both his ride and from trying to talk to her.

He slept. When he awoke it was already dark outside. He washed the sleep from his eyes, dressed and went down, seeking something to eat. In his present mood he avoided the hotel dining room for fear of meeting Clara, and ate in a small restaurant at the end of the block. Afterward he turned toward the saloon.

Half a dozen townsmen lounged at the bar and a single poker game progressed in the rear. Ford sat in his accustomed place, his back against the wall, facing the street, but he did not look up until his half-brother paused at his side.

When he did surprise twisted his carefully schooled features. "Who ran you through the meat grinder?"

Dale knew that everyone in the room was watching him. He did not know how much of the story had gotten out, and he did not want it repeated here.

"Come on, take a walk."

"Later."

"I may not be here later."

Ford glanced at him sharply, then with a shrug of resignation pushed back his chair. No one spoke as the two brothers paced the length of the bar and stepped into the darkness of the street.

Ford walked to the corner, glanced both ways. There were half a dozen horses at the long racks but not a soul in sight in either direction.

"Okay, who beat you up?"

Dale told him everything that had happened from his meeting with Arthur. Ford listened. Halfway through the recital he pulled a cigar and lit it, the flare of the match showing up his lean face momentarily in the tiny glow.

He flipped the match away, saying only, "I warned you that you're too soft to fight King. Now you've got that crazy Russian down on your neck too. You'd best ride out."

"I'm going."

Ford was surprised. "You mean you're folding so easily? Where's all this wild talk of fighting King?"

"I'm leaving town tonight, but I'm not leaving the country. I thought I ought to talk to you before I go. I thought we should have an understanding."

Ford's voice sharpened a little. "An understanding about what, dear brother?"

Dale held his temper with effort. Ford could always rub him the wrong way. He said flatly, "I'm going to take it away from King. I'm going to prove that it was always mine."

Ford turned to face him squarely. Only the glowing coal of the cigar as he puffed rapidly showed emotion. "And where does that leave me?"

"That's what I want to talk about. None of this is your fault, and you are my brother. As far as I am concerned, if you will pitch in and help you can have half the ranch."

The cigar coal continued to wink. "A very interesting proposition." Ford sounded a little mocking now. "And very generous of you, I might add, which only confirms in my mind that you aren't very smart. But look at it this way. King and I don't get along, yet under the terms of Ma's will the ranch is only his for his lifetime. Then it comes to us. Personally, I think you're wasting a lot of time and effort. If you want to hurry things along you could always kill King."

Dale regarded him for a long space in silence, then without further words he turned on his heel and moved back toward the hotel. Behind him the night was cut by Ford's taunting laughter.

In his room he hastily threw together his gear, strapping it in a tight roll bound by his slicker. He swung it to his shoulder and again went down the stairs. There was no one in sight so he tapped the hand bell.

He heard Clara's steps cross the dining room, and saw the surprise change her eyes when she noticed the bed roll. "Dale, you're not leaving?"

He nodded. "I came for my bill."

She hesitated, then picking up the pen, figured it. "But I thought . . ."

"You thought I was going to fight King? I am."

"Then why . . . ?"

He said grimly, "I need help, and I've figured out that it isn't the smartest thing for me to stay in Climax. Either King will try to set up another ambush or the big Russian will decide he needs some more exercise."

He laid money on the desk and started away.

Impulsively she put a hand on his arm. Clara Austin was not a woman who liked having a man walk away from her, any man, if there was the slightest possibility that he might be of use to her.

"Dale, wait. You're going away angry with me."

He looked down at her and her gray-green eyes seemed almost black in the shallow lamplight. "What difference does it make?"

She was almost pleading now. "Understand what I'm up against, Dale. What can a woman do in this dreary country? I can't ever hope to get away unless King helps me."

The quick thought crossed his mind that Lucy Colton was standing alone, not asking odds because she was a woman, not asking for sympathy or aid.

But he put the thought aside consciously almost as soon as it came. The situations were different. Lucy Colton was the owner of a huge ranch. She had a brother, even if he were hardly full grown, even if he and his sister failed to see eye to eye.

And the girls were different. There was a hard core of self-reliance in Lucy. She would never in the world turn to any man for assistance.

Clara was weaker, more dependent on outside help. Perhaps that was what attracted him so strongly—his awareness that she needed protection, even from herself. The impulse came without thought.

He leaned forward suddenly and kissed her hard, so hard that it made his bruised lips burn. Then he turned and strode down the long room, conscious that she called his name with a note of despairing urgency.

The night swallowed him. He glanced back once, but she had not followed him to the lighted doorway. He moved along the street, far more cautious than he had been when he had first ridden back into Climax. He had, he thought with bitterness, learned the hard way. This town which had been his home had become a trap, baited with danger. At any moment violence could sweep out at him from any direction.

He heard horses just before he reached the livery, and stepped into the shade of a dark doorway to watch four men ride past. He could not tell in the gloom whether they were Thunderhead or Colton, or stray riders from the outer reaches of the range, and he had no intention of trying to learn.

At the livery he roused the sleepy hostler, saddled his animal and rode out through the rear door, followed the rutted alley until it reached the bank of the river, then moved along that to the bridge and so gained the rising trail beyond.

He rode steadily yet without hurry, preferring to conserve the horse's strength for later use. His course took him along the Tapline road, to turn off half a dozen miles south of Thunderhead's main buildings into the track which led across the rolling grasslands toward the opening of Squaw Canyon.

Every foot he traveled was familiar ground. This was the heart of Thunderhead. It stretched around him, a million acres of lush, well-watered grass, a reservoir of wealth hardly paralleled anywhere in the west. Certainly it was worth fighting for.

He saw bunches of cattle in the light of the late moon only now lifting its pale face above the tree-shrouded hills, but it seemed to his knowing eye that there were far fewer than he remembered. The winter kill had apparently taken a heavy toll.

It was near daylight when he came, at last, to the canyon mouth and headed upward into country which could not be considered part of Thunderhead.

Here were mountain valleys offering good feed for most of the year. These valleys had been pre-empted by hill people who built their cabins, ran their few head of stock and eked out a threadbare existence with a little hunting, a little trapping, a little panning in the creeks, and an occasional Thunderhead steer that may have wandered into the higher reaches.

These were the people he wanted to reach, whom he hoped to weld to his cause. He would promise them that once in control of Thunderhead he would reverse the hard policy by which King

Parson had harassed his less fortunate neighbors. The public land used so long by Thunderhead as a God-given right would again be thrown open.

He camped in a side canyon, where a thin stream broke out from under the rock face and cut downward rapidly to join the boiling waters of Squaw Creek.

His bedground was high enough above the main canyon that anyone passing through would not see him. He slept until the sun, slanting down, struck his eyes. He had no watch but he judged that it must be nearing noon.

He was ravenously hungry, but he had no food. He washed in the creek, the chill waters soothing the multicolored bruises mottling his body.

Afterward he mounted and traveled up the canyon. It was nearly five when the land widened into a meadow a thousand acres in extent, studded with aspen and pole pine. Through them the road led to a collection of buildings that had housed a tie camp twenty-five years before, when the railroad crossed the range for the first time.

Most of the buildings stood vacant, their windows like empty eyes from which the pupils have been removed. But the square log store still boasted a faded sign and there were four horses tied to the swayback hitching rack.

Dale glanced at the brands as he rode up, noting that none of them carried the irregular triangle of Thunderhead or the IC of the Coltons. In fact, only one horse at the rail was branded at all, and this was a mark Dale had never seen before.

He stepped down from his tired animal, looped the reins and climbed to the broken, unsheltered gallery running below the dusty windows of the store.

The door stuck, and he pushed it open with difficulty to emerge into a large room, so cluttered that it looked more like a secondhand establishment than a place selling everyday merchandize.

There was a fat man behind the far counter. Four others loafed before the whiskey barrel which sat on its own shelf at the rear of the store. They all held tin cups and it was clear that they had been drinking, and that for some reason of their own they resented Dale's arrival.

They watched him with ill-concealed hostility, drawing unconsciously together as if they found comfort in their own numbers.

Dale, after a single glance, ignored them. He walked to the low counter and stopped before the fat man.

"Don't you remember me, Pops?"

Pops Jordan squinted at him through small, near-sighted eyes. "Seems like I've seen you somewhere, son, but I can't be sure."

"Dale Thorne."

It took a full minute for the name to register with Jordan. "By damn. King Parson's stepson."

A stir shifted the men around the whiskey barrel. One taller than the rest, with sun-faded hair and sandy brows so light as to hardly show against his sun-reddened skin, stepped forward.

His walk was a loose-jointed motion that somehow reminded Dale of a crane, and there was nothing impressive about him from his hatchet face to the flat, starved stomach and fleshless hips.

"Did you say King Parson's stepson?"

Jordan was beaming happily. "That's right. Best boy I ever saw. Used to ride up here when he was a little shaver and bring me a mess of fish."

"We don't need no Parsons in this country." The tall man had the dregs of his drink in the tin cup. He heaved it with an underhand toss, aimed at Dale's eyes.

Dale ,saw the whiskey coming. He ducked sidewise and drove his right hand into the thin man's stomach, then hooked a wicked left to the jaw.

The man sat down, hard, but Dale had already swung half around, drawing his gun, settling the sights on the other three riders near the barrel.

"Anyone else asking for part of this?"

They stood immobile, their faces made stupid by surprise. The man on the floor moved and Dale backed three steps to cover him as well as his companions.

Pops Jordan said in a scared voice, "He don't

mean nothing, Dale. The Thunderhead crew hung his brother last month. He don't feel exactly kindly to your stepfather. You can understand that."

Dale looked down at the man, at the thin face, at the long, thin jaw. Then he stepped forward, reached down, got a hand under the man's armpit and lifted him to his shaky legs.

"You've got no fight with me, but the next time you jump a stranger, know what you're doing before you get hurt."

The man stared at him sullenly. "I want no truck with Parson or any of his murdering breed."

"Neither do I. That's what I rode up here for."

The man's long jaw dropped. "I don't get you."

Dale spoke without turning, the gun still held loosely in his fist. "You tell them, Pops. Maybe they might believe you where they wouldn't believe me."

Jordan sounded uncertain. He was a man who hated trouble and had managed to avoid it most of his life. "What do you want me to tell them, Dale?"

"The full story." Dale watched the men. Every one of them wore guns and he judged that they could be dangerous. "Tell them how Parson married my mother. Tell them that he crowded me out of my home."

"That's right." The fat man seemed relieved that his path had been charted for him. "It's the gospel so help me. This boy used to come riding up here with whip marks on his back that I'd hate to see on a stubborn mule. King Parson's a devil. We all know it. Especially the people who live in these hills. There ain't a man within a hundred miles who hasn't seen Thunderhead ride through scattering his stock, cutting his fences, scaring hell out of his wife and children."

There was a low growl from around the barrel, as if one of the drinkers was adding his say-so to that of the storekeeper.

"But you think you had it bad? You had nothing like this kid did. Parson hated him. Dale never lived at the big house. Most of the time he would have starved if it hadn't been for the cook and crew. Don't think he's a friend of King Parson. I'll vouch for him. He ain't."

Dale said, "Thanks, Pops."

The fat man sounded aggrieved. "Don't thank me. A man's got no right to be thanked for telling the simple truth. I never expected to see you back in this country. What happened to your face?"

Dale took another look at the watchful men, then made a small ceremony of dropping his gun back into place, by so doing assuring them all that the trouble was over.

"It's a long story, Pops, and a dry one. I'll buy a drink."

The fat man moved around the end of the

counter and over to the whiskey barrel. He took down a battered cup, let an inch of whiskey run into it and passed it to Dale.

"On the house. What are you doing up here, Dale?"

"Looking for men."

They watched him, not understanding. The man he had hit stood fingering his sore jaw.

Dale told them then, about meeting DuBois in California, about coming home to reclaim the ranch, about Les's death and his own beating at the hands of the Colton crew.

"So I need help."

"And why should we help you?" It was the tall blond man.

Pops Jordan said, "Seems to me, Boyer, you'd be the first to offer. You been shooting off your face plenty ever since your brother got hung. You said all you wanted was a chance at King Parson."

The man did not look at him. His voice was truculent. "I asked him, not you."

"All right," said Dale. "I know these hills, and a lot of the people in them know me. I know none of you have it very good. I'll need a crew when I take back the ranch, and I'll pick my crew from the men who help me now. The rest of you, those with the small ranches, need winter feed and graze. I'm offering to throw Thunderhead open to all your stock. There's feed enough to share, and we'll round up the cattle spring and fall and sort them.

"I'll even go further than that. Most of you don't raise enough critters to pay you to drive to the railroad. You either have to sell to one of the cattle buyers who come through or butcher your stock for your own use. I'll promise that we'll make the drive together, and each man will be paid his share of the tally at the railroad."

"That," said Jordan, "is one of the fairest offers I ever heard." His eyes were already glinting. Dale knew what was passing through the fat man's mind. Most of his slender trade was drawn out of these hills. If conditions improved for his customers, they would improve for him.

But it went deeper. This untidy fat man was one of the kindest people Dale had ever known. The hill ranchers looked up to him, came to him with their troubles, making him a kind of unofficial judge of their disputes, accepting his rulings as if they were backed up by law.

Dale had counted on this, knowing that if Jordan backed him even the brush outlaws—the men who weren't above running off a few head of stock—would listen. For these semi-fugitives well knew that they remained safe in their wooded canyons only so long as the hill people did not drive them out at Jordan's order.

Boyer grunted. "If we can believe him."

Jordan swung on him, and some of the authority

which he exercised rang in his voice. "Can you believe me?"

"You could be mistaken. He's still from Thunderhead."

"Didn't you hear what he said? He is Thunderhead." Jordan turned to face Dale. "Don't pay any attention to him. He's more mouth than performance. Don't worry. I'll round up a crew. You don't need the likes of Clem Boyer."

"Now wait a minute!" Boyer reached over and spilled liquor into a new cup. He drank deeply, wiping his slash of a mouth with the back of his hand. "I say something, I mean it. I want a crack at King Parson. I just wanted to be sure. Count me in."

Dale looked him over. The man was as unprepossessing as any he had ever seen. His clothes were patched, stained; his sallow cheeks carried a two-day-old stubble of beard, and his mouth seemed weak. But he looked back at Dale directly, almost defiantly, his eyes steady and hard with purpose.

Dale stuck out his hand. "All right." He made a quick decision then. This man had purpose behind his actions. He hated Parson personally. Dale said, "You're my foreman."

Jordan started to protest, but after looking first at Dale, then at Boyer, he changed his mind. The man's thin, slightly stooped shoulders had straightened, his chin was suddenly up, and he said in a voice which had the edge of wonder in it,

"You hear that? Foreman of Thunderhead." From his tone he might suddenly have been elected governor of the state. He could not have been more impressed.

"Not yet," said Dale. "You'll have to help me take it first."

"We'll take it." There was a strident ring to Boyer's voice. "We'll take it if we have to kill every gunman in that crew."

CHAPTER TEN

It looked like Fair Day. There were more people in the old tie camp at one time than anyone had ever seen before. An air of festivity marked the gathering. Whole families had driven down out of their canyon homesteads, bringing the children, bringing their lunches. People who had not seen each other in months gathered into groups, exchanging news and gossip.

Pops Jordan had set the whiskey barrel on a corner of the store porch, and it was free to all at Dale's expense. But Jordan kept a watchful eye on the dispensing, storing in his machine-like memory the number of drinks each visitor had, refusing them after their third cup.

"We didn't come here to have a brawl," he told them finally after they had gathered in a semi-circle before the porch. "This is a serious business and it can affect you all."

They attended him and Dale, standing at his side, studied the solid, weatherbeaten faces: the women bent from work in their faded dresses and bonnets, the kids, barefooted and often dirty, and he thought how little they have, and I'm here asking them to fight for me when they have never been able to fight for themselves.

They all knew why they were there. The

riders Pops Jordan had sent out with word of the meeting had told them varying versions of what to expect.

That they had come at all showed their interest, but he knew that it would take more than interest to stand against Thunderhead's trained guns.

"I won't waste your time." It was still Pops talking. "I'll let Dale tell you what is on his mind."

He walked away then to sit heavily beside the whiskey barrel, his short body almost as rounded as the keg he leaned against.

Dale took a long breath. This was the first time in his life he had ever attempted to make a speech, and suddenly he experienced a sensation of fright. What if he failed to reach them, to make them understand? When he had first thought of enlisting their aid it had seemed very simple. Now, standing here he could not actually believe that he could convince anyone.

Then he noticed Boyer in the crowd, behind a slender woman in a dress so often washed that the pattern had all but faded out. Boyer winked at him, as if they stood shoulder to shoulder against this moment.

That wink gave Dale the confidence he needed. He cleared his throat and began speaking in a voice which steadied and grew stronger as he continued,

"A lot of you knew me and were kind to

me when I was a boy. You know the story of Thunderhead, and of King Parson as well or better than I do. Most of you have felt King's heavy hand."

There was a murmur through the crowd.

He went on to tell then of meeting DuBois in California, of learning of the will which left the ranch to him. "I mean to find that will. I mean to take back the ranch. When I do, I'll throw the valley open to all your cattle. It is, after all, government land."

The murmur of voices rose in volume. This was a sore point with them, running back to his father's time.

"But to do this I need a fighting crew. Before we are finished I'm afraid we'll have to battle not only Thunderhead but also Lucy Colton.

"I want thirty men. I'd rather they be unmarried. I'll pay forty dollars a month and found, but I can't pay now. I have five hundred dollars. That will go for food and shells. You will have to furnish your own horses.

"Those who are interested talk to Clem Boyer. He is my foreman. Now, if you will step over to the barrel Pops will pour one drink all around. And let me say this: when I get the ranch the use of the grass will not be restricted to those who fight with me. It is for us all. This country is changing. The days when a big ranch dominates a territory are passing. You and I will live to

114

see the valley fenced, to see Thunderhead much smaller than it is today.

"All I want is to build a community where we can live in peace, where a man doesn't have to look across his shoulder before he rides over a hill."

He stepped down. For a moment no one in the crowd moved, then as if by common impulse they flooded around him, everyone trying to talk at once.

The story of his fight with the Russian was all through the hills. A dozen women came up to clasp his hand, to invite him to their homesteads to stay.

Pops Jordan and his riders had sold the idea well, and before sundown he had his crew, gathered around Clem Boyer talking plans, discussing where they would get horses.

Dale selected the old building which had once served as a bunkhouse for the tie cutters as headquarters. He put the crew, under Boyer, to cleaning out the place, cutting boughs to use as mattresses for the plank bunks, organizing a cook house, and buying supplies from Jordan.

He and the fat man were in the store alone, going over the list, when Dale thought of something that had not crossed his mind before.

"There's one thing about this I don't like, Pops."

The fat man had been totaling the bill. He

looked up, his round eyes inquiring. "What's that, Bronco?"

"Maybe we shouldn't move into the old bunkhouse. When King finds out I'm up here he'll likely send a crew to try to burn the place, and they are apt to jump this store at the same time."

Jordan shrugged. "They'd better send a full crew. It ain't been safe the last couple of years for a lone Thunderhead rider to venture too far into these hills. If he sends up a crew he's likely to find not only the men who signed on with you, but every dang man in the canyons waiting for them. Yes, and the women too. You've got them stirred up as nothing else ever did. They're ready to fight. I think they'd fight now even if you didn't stay to see it through. They've been kicked and pummeled and chased so long they just won't take much more. But you give me an idea. I'm going to corral some of the boys—not the ones who are riding with you, but the others. We'll set up a kind of lookout system. They can squat on some of the hills and watch. The Indians used smoke signals, why can't we?"

He went out to where the ranchers were beginning to harness their teams for the long drives home, and asked for volunteers.

Sitting around the open fire, with the new group gathered about him, Dale had to admit that they were as sorry a looking bunch as he had ever seen. There was hardly a man whose shirt had not been patched in a dozen places, and the way they attacked the food showed that few of them had had enough to eat in years.

His money would not go far or last long at this rate, and they needed meat.

He called Boyer over and said shortly, "From now on we start eating Thunderhead beef."

The man's eyes flickered wide, then a grin split his narrow face. "You hear that, fellows?" He raised his voice. "Boss says we start eating Thunderhead beef."

There was a swell of talk.

"We're all going to ride down the canyon in half an hour. No use waiting. Twenty-five of you are going on to Climax with me. The other five go with Boyer and round up twenty head of the first stock we hit and drive them back up the canyon. We can throw them out on grass here and butcher them as they are needed."

One of the men beyond the fire said, "That'll stir King up for sure."

Dale shrugged. "King is going to be too busy thinking of other things to even realize a few steers have vanished. Okay, we ride in ten minutes."

They rode, Boyer at his side, the rest stringing out behind in a double line. The canyon road was too narrow in most places for more to travel abreast.

Boyer said, "And if it isn't too much to ask, why are you riding into Climax? Looking for a fight?"

Dale shook his head. "Aside from using a few of my own cows to keep us fed, I want to keep this business as legal as possible. I want a copy of my father's will."

"Where is it?"

"I'd guess Ben Underwood has it hid somewhere, knowing Ben. He's a cautious soul who plays his cards close to his vest. I always wondered why King kept him in office all these years, since King never had much use for him. Now I know. Underwood had the will to hold over him."

"This gets you in trouble with the law."

Dale looked at him. "You didn't really expect the law to give us any help, did you?"

"No."

"Then what are you worrying about?"

Boyer grinned in the darkness. "Hell, I ain't worrying. I'm just talking. It's worth living, just to see King Parson's face when you drag him into court."

They found cattle scattered across the grass within half a mile of the canyon mouth, and the whole crew helped to round up twenty head, and Boyer with five men headed them up the canyon. The rest rode for Climax.

Dale knew that they ran the chance of meeting

Thunderhead men, but they were heavily armed and the riders behind him were spoiling for a battle.

Yet they met no one, coming down through Loud Canyon and crossing the bridge at a walk so that the pound of their hoofs on the hollow board bridge would not disturb the town.

Dale turned and led the way along the alley, warning the men to remain quiet until they reached the rear of the courthouse. Here he ringed them about the building, so that if there was any disturbance, any attempt at help from the outside, they would be ready.

Main Street was deserted, the lights in the hotel lobby off. In fact, the Palace Saloon was the only building which showed any signs of life, and he judged that the nightly poker game was still in session, that Ford would probably be in his usual place.

He grinned to himself as he turned toward the entrance of the sheriff's quarters, thinking of what Ford's reaction would be when he heard of this night's work.

He knocked on the door, waited and knocked again. Finally there was movement inside, a light was lit and Underwood's voice called through the door.

"Who is it? What's the matter?"

"It's Dale, Uncle Ben. There's been trouble at Thunderhead."

He heard Underwood swear, heard him fumble with the catch, then the door swung back to expose the sheriff in his nightshirt.

"What kind of trouble?"

Dale put a hand against his chest and pushed him gently but firmly backward into the room, stepping after him, followed by three of his men.

The sheriff sputtered in surprise. "What is this, Bronco?"

Dale said shortly, "The will. My father's will, remember? I want it."

Underwood recovered himself and his old face set in stern lines. "You're crazy. DuBois lied to you. There never was such a will."

"I think there was, Uncle Ben." Dale's tone was low but carried an edge to his words which the sheriff had never heard there before. "We haven't much time, so let's not waste it. Where is the will?"

"You'll get in trouble for this." Underwood decided to bluster.

"Not much more trouble than I'm already in. I've got twenty-five men with me, Uncle Ben. None of them like King Parson and I doubt if any of them care very much for you."

Underwood stared at him. He looked at the grim faces behind Thorne, at the drawn guns.

"Where did you get twenty-five men?"

"I've got more than that, as King is going to find out. You bet on the wrong side, Uncle Ben. It must have looked easy, years ago . . . a small boy. King Parson in the saddle and you in the sheriff's office as long as you kept the will over his head. I want it now."

Underwood was jumpy. His eyes held a haunted look. Nothing like this had ever happened to him before. He had grown fat and contented and lazy behind the sheriff's star. There never was much trouble in the country. King Parson's heavy hand had kept it down, until a couple of years ago when Lucy Colton had taken over from her father and started to hire gun hands.

Then King Parson had gotten desperate when he could no longer drive his shippers across Colton range, had started hiring guns of his own.

Underwood had known then that his days of easy peace were numbered, but like most people who have made office holding their career he had vacillated, putting off day by day the knowledge that sooner or later there would be an explosion, and that he would have to take sides.

What he had not expected was any real action from Dale Thorne. He still considered him as a defenseless boy, frightened by King Parson, keeping as much as possible out of the rancher's way.

"Who says I still have it?" As soon as the words were out he realized the slip he had made, but it was then too late.

Dale Thorne laughed. It chilled Underwood

more than any threat would have. This was not the boy he had known, this was a stranger, turned hard and relentless by three years of wandering.

"You have it. I'm going to take it."

"You're wrong, Dale. There never was a will." He continued the lie, caught in an ugly mesh and not knowing what else to do.

The inner door opened and Mrs. Underwood stuck her gray head through the opening. "Ben, what is it?" Then she saw Dale and relief eased the wrinkles in her face. "Oh, Dale. I didn't know what was going on. I . . ." She stopped, gasping at the grim-faced men behind Thorne, at the drawn guns, and fear came back to her dark eyes.

"Dale, what is it? What are you trying to do?"

His voice gentled, for he liked Virginia Underwood. "Go back in the other room, Ma'am. We've just a little business with the sheriff."

"But who are these men? Why the guns?"

He said steadily, "Go back in the other room. Nothing will happen to Ben if he is reasonable."

"Reasonable?"

The sheriff sounded despairing. "Virginia, he's lost his mind. He thinks his father made a will before he died, giving Thunderhead to him, not to his mother. He thinks I have that will."

She threw a bitter glance at Dale. "I'll get help." She turned back toward the door.

Dale said, "I've got twenty men outside. They won't let you through, Ma'am."

She turned again to stare at him in contempt. "Would you fight an old woman?"

"Not unless you make me. I didn't think up this situation."

For the first time it seemed to occur to her that there might be something in what Dale was saying. She looked for a long minute at her husband. When she spoke it was in a tender, inquiring voice.

"Ben, is there such a will?"

He swung to face her angrily, bluster still in his harried voice. "You would ask me a thing like that?"

She kept looking at him steadily, and under the gaze his eyes dropped. "I . . . well . . ."

"Get it for him, Ben." The words were still soft, but the tone had grown commanding.

"You'd take his word against mine?"

"Get it for him, Ben."

The sheriff stood for an instant longer, then his shoulders sagged. A beaten man, he moved toward the big old-fashioned safe in the corner of the office. He knelt, his bare ankles looking skinny, almost fleshless, and spun the heavy dial. No one said anything. Mrs. Underwood met Dale's eyes levelly, then lowered hers to the floor at his feet.

Somehow the look cut Dale more than anything that could have happened. He knew what he had done this night, and if it had been within his power he would have tried to undo it. He had destroyed a woman's faith in the man with whom she had lived for almost fifty years.

The sheriff had the safe open. He rummaged through its contents and straightened, holding an envelope. He stood looking down at it, then turned silently and extended it to Thorne. There were tears in his eyes.

"I'm sorry, Dale."

Thorne took the envelope and drew out the folded sheet it contained and glanced over it. It was short and to the point. Dan Thorne left his wife one dollar and the right to live at the ranch for the rest of her life. The ranch itself was left to "Dale Thorne, my son, his interests and safety to be watched after by Ben Underwood, serving as trustee until said Dale Thorne reaches the age of twenty-one."

Dale could not remember his father's signature, but he had no doubt that the awkward scrawl was authentic.

Slowly he looked up at the sheriff. "Why, Uncle Ben?"

Ben Underwood walked away heavily and sank into the chair beside the desk.

"You ask me why. Why is a man born a coward? Why can't he live up to the things he believes in? King Parson came to me the day after your father died. He said he knew about the will. He said he wanted it.

"I refused to give it to him. Then he told me that he meant to marry your mother, that he meant to have the ranch. He said he'd kill me if I ever mentioned the will. He would have, too. I told him DuBois had drawn the will, that even if I were willing to go along, DuBois would expose us. He said he would attend to DuBois."

He looked up at Dale, pleading in his old eyes. "There's one other thing, boy, that cinched it for me. I knew King Parson for what he is—an inhuman bully. And you were a little boy. If that will were made public, your life wouldn't have been worth a plugged nickel. You'd have been found dead the week after your mother married King."

The old voice broke. Mrs. Underwood moved over and put her arm around the sheriff's shaking shoulders.

"Thanks," said Dale. "Thanks for that part, Uncle Ben." He walked to him and laid a hand on the back of the bowed neck, then turned and left the room. This hurt him more than the knowledge that for years he had been deprived of what belonged to him.

Outside the men crowded around him in jubilation. Those who had accompanied him into the sheriff's office passed the word.

He merely nodded in reply to their shouts of congratulations. He walked to his horse, mounted

125

and rode down the street, his men following. He stepped down before the Palace Saloon and, telling them to wait, moved through the swinging doors into the long room.

Ford was at his table. Five men were playing with him, but aside from them and the sleepy bartender the place was empty.

Ford looked up as he came in, and his eyebrows climbed. Dale did not go back to the table. Instead he veered to the bar, motioning. Ford left his chips, saying, "Deal me out for a couple of hands," and came to the bar.

The bartender moved forward but Dale shook his head and the man went back to the week-old newspaper he had been studying with half-closed eyes.

"You didn't stay long."

Dale said, "I just came in to get this." Silently he handed Ford the folded will.

His brother read it twice, no change of expression on his handsome face. Then he refolded it, but made no move to return it.

"Where'd you get it?"

"From Ben Underwood. It's been in his safe all these years."

"What are you going to do with it?"

"Haul King into court. Dispossess him of the ranch."

Ford was silent, thinking. "And what happens to me?"

Dale told him, "I offered you a deal the other night. It still goes."

Ford was laughing quietly. "You know, if the boot were on the other foot, what I'd do to you?"

"Maybe."

"No maybe about it. The milk of human kindness is not a major portion of my makeup. But if you hadn't offered, I'd still be around with my hand out."

"Then you're with me?"

Ford returned the will slowly. "Let's say that I'm not against you. You haven't whipped King yet."

"I've made a good start."

"You've made a start. How good it is I'll tell you later. I suppose you did not come here merely for the pleasure of looking at my charming features? I suppose you want something?"

"The name of a lawyer in this county with nerve enough to go up against King."

"Hm. That poses a problem. Still, Dick Styles has only been in the county a year. He might take your case."

"Where will I find him?"

Ford said, "Always at hand, as long as the cards are dealt or the whiskey flows." He turned his head and called across the room. "Dick, come over here a minute."

A tall man looked their way. He was black-

127

haired, hawk-faced, and Dale judged him not too much older than himself.

He said, "In a minute," and played out the hand, losing to three kings. Then he rose and sauntered rather than walked to the bar.

Ford said, "Meet my brother. I think you saw him the other night when he so gallantly grabbed the whip that vixen was using on me."

Dick Styles nodded. He sported a slow, secretive smile as if he found the whole world vastly amusing and refused to take it with any degree of seriousness.

"My brother thinks he has a case for you if you aren't afraid to go up against my dad."

Styles's shrug was expressive. "I'd go up against the devil himself for a proper fee. If you keep winning my money at poker I'll need a case bad."

"I'm worried about you." Ford was ironic as he turned to Dale. "I never saw him lose but once since he's been here. Show him the will, Dale."

Thorne handed over the will. Styles read it twice, then began to ask questions. Dale told him the full story in a dozen sentences.

"So the sheriff held this out all this time?"

"That's right."

"And do you think he'll get up on the stand and testify in your favor when he's admitting to the world that he was party to the swindle?"

"I think he will."

"Why?"

"Because of his wife. Because she knew nothing about it, and she was horrified when she found out tonight. If it hadn't been for her I suspect I'd have had to blow that safe to get it."

Styles whistled softly. "Women, women, never underestimate them or guess what they may do. You may be right at that. If you will leave this with me I'll file action."

Dale hesitated for a moment in silence. All he knew about this lawyer was that he played poker with Ford. This could be one of Ford's traps, a way to get the will, to make his own deal with King.

"I'll produce it when the time comes."

Ford's laugh was amused. "Not so trustful any longer, are you?"

"I'm learning," Dale said, and left them, going back into the night.

CHAPTER ELEVEN

Word of the suit ran through the valley like wildfire, and court day saw the whole countryside drained into Climax. King Parson rode up heading a party of twenty-five men. They made a flourish of arriving, and stomped into the courtroom as a body.

Dale came, with not only his thirty men but also a good additional fifty hill people, these drawn by curiosity and their hope of gain if Thunderhead should pass into his possession. They were just dismounting before the courthouse when the Coltons appeared, Lucy and Vince in front, fifteen of their crew trailing along.

Ford sauntered toward him as Dale ducked under the hitch rail, and stopped to look at his brother sardonically.

"Looks like the makings of a war. I've never seen so many men or guns in this town in my life." He turned, sweeping off his hat as Lucy Colton, ahead of Vince, crossed the street from the rack where they had tied their horses.

"Good morning. I hardly recognized you without your whip."

She looked him over coldly. "It's a shame you aren't paid for your wit, Ford."

He bowed. "But I am, dear lady. It is my wits which keep me alive at the poker table. Ask your brother there if you don't believe me."

Dale expected Vince to resent the remark. Instead he winked at Ford. "I can sure vouch for that."

Lucy started to move on to the stairs, but Ford sidestepped to block her path.

"I'm curious." He was still smiling faintly. "I know why King brought a lot of his riders with him, and Dale seems to have combed the hills for every rag-tail rancher he could find. But what about you? Did you come in to join the fight or merely to referee?"

She said, "You think there will be a fight?"

"If King loses the case, of course. The only way you'll ever get him off Thunderhead is to carry him, feet first."

"We'll see."

"Or have you joined Dale? I understand you played nurse for him when your handy man nearly killed him." Ford's glance upon her was sardonic and mocking.

Lucy's eyes went to Dale inquiringly, noting the marks of the beating still plain on his face.

"You didn't waste much time." There was a note of grudging admiration in her voice. "I didn't think you could dig up a crew—certainly not that many men."

He said, "They aren't all my crew. Some are

131

merely friends, the others are people who just don't like King."

"I'm still surprised that they ride with you. I wonder what you promised them."

"Nothing very startling," Dale retorted, "just a chance to run their stock on valley grass during the winter."

"You didn't!" Ford spun on his brother, and for once in his life Ford was entirely serious and the perpetual, mocking grin was gone. "Let them run on Thunderhead?"

"Why not? It's public range. With the number of cows any of them have it will be years before the grass is over-grazed. And things are changing. We'll have to learn to change with them if we hope to survive. No territory can get along with one or two big ranches brow-beating and intimidating their neighbors."

Lucy Colton was watching him with speculation in her eyes. "This isn't a trick? A way of getting them to help you and later crushing them one by one?"

He said harshly, "It's no trick. I figure there is grass enough for all of us."

"I never expected to hear a Thorne say a thing like that."

Ford's voice was tight and angry. "I didn't either. I think he's gone crazy."

"Think what you like. That's the way it is."

"Then maybe I'd better string along with

King," Ford snapped. "I should have known there was a catch to it when you so generously offered to share the ranch with me. If you keep giving it away there will be nothing left to share." He swung around and stalked up the courthouse steps.

Lucy watched Ford go, then turned to Dale. "It seems that nothing you do makes you very popular with anyone. I'll try to keep my men from causing trouble, but I couldn't keep them from riding in."

Beyond her Dale saw the Russian's hulking form and the half sneer on the man's heavy lips. He said in a low tone, "Does that mean you've changed your mind, that if the court gives me Thunderhead the fight is off between us?"

She said slowly, "The hills will still mark the boundary. What you do north of them is your affair. South is mine." She brushed past him then and went up the steps, and he found himself facing Sarcoff.

The man's lips pulled back from his yellow teeth in a wicked grimace. "I told you next time we meet I kill you. You wouldn't listen."

Dale's voice held an edge of contempt. "Don't try it. I can put three bullets in you before you can get to that gun. And as for potting at my back, I've got nearly a hundred men with me. They'd like nothing better than to string you up, and every man of your crew with you. So keep out of my way."

He paced directly toward Sarcoff, for he had seen his lawyer coming and wanted to speak to him. The Russian held his ground until Thorne was within a step, then he raised a big fist.

Dale Thorne wasted no motion. He drew his colt and jabbed the barrel an inch into Sarcoff's belly, at the same time slapping him across the eyes with his free hand.

"Try it and I'll blow a hole in you. Now back out of my way."

For a moment Dale thought the giant would refuse, seeing the hate flare up in the black eyes. Then Sarcoff stepped to one side and Dale's men closed about him, ringing him in, facing the Colton crew, making it very plain that if the men from the south end of the valley were looking for trouble they had found it.

The tension held for a full minute, then the Colton riders veered away and headed for the Palace Saloon, Sarcoff the last to give ground.

Dale had met the lawyer, and Styles watched the two groups of men with amusement. "Only a spark," he said in his soft voice, "and this street would be filled with death."

Dale nodded. "What about the trial? Is everything set? Will the sheriff testify?"

"He will testify," said Styles. "You were right about his wife. She's a strong-willed woman with a stern sense of justice. I spent an hour with them last night. Ben Underwood is scared. He's like a rabbit looking for a hole to hop into, but he will testify."

"All right. Let's go in."

They turned, walking between two ordered lines of Dale Thorne's men to the steps, then passed into the building. Ten of the crew, acting on orders, followed them inside. The rest, under Boyer, spread out around the front of the courthouse, primed and ready for trouble.

Dale and the lawyer walked down the center aisle of the courtroom, ignoring the catcalls of Thunderhead men ranged in the rows of seats on each side of the aisle, and found their places behind the counsel table to the left of the bench.

They were hardly seated when the clerk of the court bustled in to call the session to order. Then the door behind the bench opened and the judge appeared.

Thorne knew him by sight. He had been the circuit rider for this territory almost as long as Dale could remember. He took his seat, a man past middle age with a tired face and a soft smile. But he was not smiling now.

Styles rose and presented his case, a petition in probate. The judge listened without change of expression. Dale glanced around and saw Clara in the front row on the far side of the room. Lucy Colton sat three rows behind her, her eyes fixed on the judge's face. King Parson sprawled at ease, surrounded by his men. His bulky arms were folded across his barrel chest, his face expressionless, a little bored, as if this action had no bearing upon him.

Styles nudged Dale and his lips formed the word, "Will."

Dale drew the paper from his pocket and watched the lawyer carry it forward to show to the judge.

The judge read it twice, taking his time. He said finally, "I see that this was witnessed by August DuBois and Ben Underwood. I understand that the said August DuBois died last year in California."

"That is correct, Your Honor."

"And Underwood. Is he in court?"

Styles turned, expecting to find Ben Underwood seated in the witness row. He was not there.

Styles's voice took on a note of uncertainty. "I don't understand, Your Honor. He promised me he would be here."

The judge peered at him. "This is highly irregular. He is your witness."

"Yes, Your Honor. If I could have a continuance of a few minutes I'm certain I can find him."

Dale glanced at his stepfather. It seemed to him that King was smiling, although it was hard to tell. King Parson seldom showed much expression, even in his eyes.

Dale rose and walked back to the second row where he whispered some instructions to one of his men. The man rose and left the court. The judge cleared his throat.

"Since your witness is obviously not present I will grant half an hour continuance." He peered at the clerk. "I understand that this is a second will, that another will covering the estate of the deceased Daniel Thorne was filed with this court nearly twenty years ago."

"Yes, Your Honor."

"Find it in the files. Bring it here, please."

Styles had returned to the table, his face worried. "I can't understand. Underwood promised that he would be here."

"Maybe he got scared and left town. I'll have a look." Dale rose. He knew that every eye in the courtroom was on him as he made his way up the aisle to the door. Outside he nodded to Boyer and motioned him forward.

"Cover me with four or five men. I'm going to the sheriff's quarters."

He walked around the corner of the building, half of his crew following him. At the sheriff's door he paused and knocked. There was no answer.

He knocked again. Then he tried the knob. The door was unlocked and he pushed it open.

"Uncle Ben!"

Still there was no answer. Dale crossed the

front room and shoved open the bedroom door. Mrs. Underwood lay stretched on the bed, still in her nightgown, her wrists and ankles bound, a cloth gag parting her lips.

He was across the room in an instant, loosening the gag from her mouth. She tried to speak and could not, the muscles of her cheeks so strained that she could only croak.

He leaped to the door and told one of his men to find a doctor. Then he came back to release her wrists and ankles.

"Tell me what happened," he pleaded.

She tried twice before the words were understandable. "Three men—masked. They—they took Ben away."

"When?"

She tried again. "In the night. I don't know— I—" She was crying and close to hysteria.

The doctor who had been in the courtroom was out of breath when he came into the bedroom. He bent over the woman, listening to her heart. When he straightened his face was grave.

"What happened?" he asked tensely.

Dale told him swiftly and the doctor began to curse under his breath.

"Is she bad?"

"She's got a weak heart. Any kind of shock is dangerous for her." The doctor got medicine from his bag.

She was dead within the hour. Afterward

Dale decided that her passing was fortunate. It saved her added grief, for already two small boys, fishing up the river above the town, had discovered the body of Ben Underwood. The doctor, after a quick examination, declared that he had been beaten to death.

Dale had small time to worry about Mrs. Underwood's demise. News of the finding of the sheriff's body had preceded him into the courtroom, and the air was tense as he came down the aisle and again took his seat beside Styles.

The lawyer's face was grave. The judge had two papers before him and his face mirrored that of Styles. He looked up finally, letting his eyes roam across the rows of tense faces. Then he cleared his throat.

"We have here an unusual situation. The plaintiff claims that this will which he has just produced was in reality drawn later than the will which was admitted to probate some twenty years ago. Unfortunately the two men who signed as witnesses of this new will are now dead.

"The court has compared the signatures on both documents and is of the opinion that they were not signed by the same hands. In other words, this new document is declared to be fictitious and a forgery."

Dale felt his anger rise like a shock wave through him. He started to rise, but Styles already had a hand on his arm. He settled back as Styles's fingers bit into his flesh.

"There's nothing you can do," Styles told him. "Keep quiet or he will cite you for contempt."

"But there were men with me when the will was found in the safe."

"Did they see it?"

"Not to read, but . . ."

"Even if they had, it would prove nothing. It still might be a false will Underwood had. Unfortunately he cannot testify."

"Because they beat him to death—beat an old man because he was trying to right a wrong he committed long ago." Dale's face was savage with rage.

The judge was still speaking. "Therefore the plaintiff has failed to produce sufficient evidence, and I must rule in favor of the defendant. Case dismissed."

He rose, then turned and swept through the door behind the bench, closing it softly behind him.

Laughter welled up from the Thunderhead crew scattered through the room. King Parson rose. He was slyly smiling as he led his men out onto the street.

Dale got to his feet with Styles at his side, and met Lucy Colton coming from her seat.

She stopped, saying in a low voice, "I'm sorry, Dale. Truly sorry."

It startled him and he had to stammer for words. "I thought you wanted to see me lose."

"I want Thunderhead to lose. It will." She went on up the aisle, her brother following. Then Dale saw Clara standing alone at the far side of the court, and crossed to her.

"It isn't over yet."

"It is." Her voice had a dull quality he had never heard there before and her cheeks were pale. "You don't beat King, Dale. No one does."

"No," said Ford. He had come up behind Dale. "King wins again. So now you're going to marry him, Clara."

Her eyes looked very green. "Who told you that?"

"Some things," Ford said, "I can figure out without being told. You tried for Les because you wanted part of the ranch. You even looked in my direction. And you held back on King hoping that Dale would win this case. Now that he's lost you'll have to repair your bridges."

Dale swung around, reaching out to grab Ford by the edges of his carefully pressed black coat.

"Stop it if you don't want to get hurt."

"Oh, you can hurt me," Ford said. He showed no alarm. "But hitting me doesn't change anything. It doesn't even change Clara, does it, darling?"

She stared at him for a long moment, then with high head she paced from the room.

Ford looked at his brother and Dale slowly released his grip. Ford stepped back, straightening his coat.

"You know," his voice held more real warmth than Dale had known he could show. "This is about the best thing that could have happened to you. You can hit me if you want to. You don't have to believe me, but Clara is utterly no good. What she wants is important. Nothing else is."

"Let's don't talk about it," said Dale.

"There's nothing to talk about. King's won again."

"But not for long."

Ford regarded him quizzically, then shrugged and turned away.

Dale moved slowly out of the courtroom, his men forming silently around him. Across the street the Thunderhead crew had gathered before Effine's feed store, watching, mockery and challenge in the very way they stood.

The Colton crew was gone. Apparently Lucy had taken them out of town as rapidly as possible.

Dale paused on the steps. He could see King eyeing him from the opposite sidewalk with Mark Jacoby at his side. He spoke to Boyer in an undertone. "Keep the men alert."

There was no need for the warning. His crew, reinforced by the mountain ranchers, were lined along the courthouse front, their rifles ready as they hungrily watched the Thunderhead riders for signs of violence.

Boyer said in a desperate voice, "Say the word. Let's take them now."

"No, not yet."

"How long are we going to stand around, to watch King go his way, killing as he chooses? That judge was bought. He would never have been elected without King's backing."

"That's right."

"And Sheriff Ben. They beat him to death. I saw his body when it was brought in."

"We'll take care of them, but not now," Dale answered.

"Why?" The word was wrenched from Boyer by the power of his feeling.

Dale said grimly, "Because there are a lot of men standing on this sidewalk who would die. Many of them have wives and kids. Do you have any idea how many would go down if shooting started here?"

"So we ride out, our tails between our legs like always."

"No." Dale pushed through the throng before the steps and descended into the thick dust of the street. He saw that the men across from him had tensed and were watching him narrowly.

He moved slowly forward, careful to keep his hand well clear of his belted gun so that no motion of his might be misunderstood.

King had stopped talking to Jacoby and his eyes bored into those of his stepson. When Dale had reached the center of the road Parson's voice struck at him like a slashing knife.

"That's far enough!"

Dale stopped. His features were as hard as granite and there was no cringe, no fear in him. "I just wanted to tell you, King, that we aren't through. You stopped Ben Underwood from talking. What did you think—that if you beat him enough he'd testify for you?"

He waited, but King Parson had nothing to say.

"You killed him, and you killed his wife, and everyone in this valley knows it. I could say that I hope it plagues your conscience or your sleep, but I know it won't. Nothing ever has." He stopped, his voice deadly and purposeful. "But here's something for you to think about. I'm going to take what your judge cheated me out of. I'm going to take Thunderhead. Not the ranch, because that's nothing but half a dozen buildings and three sections of deeded land.

"I'm going to take all the cows Thunderhead has, and you haven't got enough men to stop me. You see these people lined up behind me here? There isn't a man among them who doesn't hate your guts. I'm telling every one of them that it is open season on your beef. I'm telling them that we'll post guards along the hills to signal if you or your crew try to ride after any of it.

"This may not help me, but it will mean that the hill people will eat better this summer than they have ever eaten in their lives. And it will break you. You're in trouble already. The winter kill thinned your stock and your fight with Lucy Colton has done you no good. You're hemmed in, King. The Coltons will jump you if you try to drive south out of here, and I'll see that you never make the railroad with a shipping herd through the hills. Think about it and think well, because you have lost Thunderhead as of this moment."

Dale turned his back then and stalked to his side of the street. His muscles crawled a little. He would not have been surprised if King had drawn his gun and shot him in the back.

But King Parson for all of his arrogant contempt of the hill people saw the line of menacing rifles and knew that if he shot Dale he would be dead before his gun ceased to smoke.

Dale came up to Boyer, saying tensely, "Let's ride."

He saw the savage smile in the man's eyes, saw it mirrored in the eyes of the brush ranchers around him. They were jubilant. For them he had in seconds turned what appeared crushing defeat into promise of a victory.

They rode out. He and Boyer held their horses while the others mounted and began to leave town. They were the last to parade before the line

145

of Thunderhead men. Not a sound issued from his stepfather's crew. Not a sound rose along the street save for the soft mush their horses' feet made in the thick dust.

CHAPTER TWELVE

They started the rustling operation that night. They did not come down the main canyon, thinking that Parson and his crew might be lying in wait for them there. Instead they worked down through the small feeder canyons, sifting out onto the range in twos and threes, picking up a few stray steers and driving them with deliberate patience through the brush and over the hogbacks to the headquarters beside Jordan's store.

It was slow work, and a week passed without noticeable results. True, they had had no clash with the Thunderhead crew, but also the cattle close to the timber seemed to be diminishing in number, and they were forced to venture further into the grasslands of the valley floor to find the animals they sought.

Dale was puzzled. Either the winter kill had been worse than he had supposed or King Parson was drifting the cows back toward the home ranch as a matter of precaution.

This was foreign to King Parson's nature. He was a man who had never consciously backed away from anything or anyone, and Dale could hardly believe that he would do so now.

On the eighth day he borrowed a pair of field glasses from Jordan and climbed a rocky promontory to the north of the mouth of Squaw Canyon, squatting there beside the hill rancher who had been designated as a lookout against attack, and training his glasses on the rolling land below him.

He saw activity almost at once. Far off across the sweep of the ranch dark figures of horsemen were gathering cattle, driving them toward the home buildings.

He sat for a long time reflecting on the story the glasses told him. The further his own men were forced to go from the screening edge of timber the more dangerous it became, and if his men tried driving cattle across the open land they would be very vulnerable to attack.

He was surprised that King had not yet attempted to attack the headquarters in the canyon. Perhaps King had been impressed by the number of armed men who had ridden in with him to the trial.

He glanced at the man beside him, then passed him the glasses and waited while the hill rancher had his careful look.

"What do you think?"

The hill man was long, lean, with a skinny neck from which an Adam's apple protruded like a rope knot.

"Looks to me like they're running a roundup."

"How many head do you think Thunderhead tallys this season?"

The man considered. He was not one who made judgments lightly or easily. "Don't rightly know. Big years they used to run nearly ten thousand head."

Dale knew this.

"Winter was bad. Deep snow, and cattle won't stomp for feed the way a horse will."

Dale was getting a little impatient with the platitudes.

"Then, too, King shipped a lot of stock last fall, lost some driving up through the canyon." Amusement glinted in the faded eyes. "Timber wolves got some of the weaker stock, so did the boys."

"Get to the point."

The man spit out the cud of tobacco he had been nursing in his hollow cheek. "Well, you asked me." He sounded defensive. "I'd say maybe he's got six or seven thousand head."

Dale nodded. He went back to his horse and rode up the winding trail, back through the hills to his headquarters. If what the lookout said was right, King Parson was in worse trouble than he had imagined.

At camp he found most of the crew asleep. Since they had been doing so much night riding they had been sleeping through most of the daylight hours. He unsaddled his horse, turned it into the small corral and walked over to look at the cattle already there.

They had gathered more than four hundred

head. Prime steers, fours and long threes. Since they could handle so few, his men had been highly selective in the stock they took, but at this rate it would take months to cripple King, and if he held the bulk of the herd around the home ranch their chances of the nightly gather would decrease day by day.

Dale turned toward the store, finding Boyer sitting on an empty keg, talking to Pops Jordan.

"Looks like King's pulling in his horns." He found a seat and helped himself to a handful of crackers from the open barrel.

They glanced at him inquiringly and he told them what he had seen.

Boyer said, "If you ask me, let's round up every man we can and strike directly at the home ranch."

"Maybe that's what King wants us to do. Whatever else he is my stepfather is no fool. We'll wait a couple of days and see what happens."

"No raid tonight?"

Dale thought about that. "Let's lay off tonight and instead you take half a dozen men and ride out for a look. See if you can learn how far back he's pushed the herd, but don't hit the main ranch and don't get into a trap. Now, I'm going to catch some sleep."

As he rose a man ran up onto the porch, shouting, and they all made for the door.

The man was pointing to Snake Mountain, a

crest on the ridge, jutting down to frown over the opening of Squaw Canyon. From the ridge a single column of smoke rose into the still afternoon air.

Pops squinted at it. "One man coming in. If there were more he'd build two fires. Wonder who's coming up."

Dale was not disturbed. It might be anyone, a chance rider, a drifter cutting through the country. All the smoke told them was that someone the lookout did not recognize, or someone identified with Thunderhead, was riding in.

They waited. Time dragged and the sun dropped lower. It would take better than two hours for the man, whoever he was, to negotiate the curving, climbing trail of the canyon.

Just before six they heard the clink of his horse's feet on the rocky trail. By that time the crew was up, gathering around the long table which the cook had fixed in the open beside the cook shack.

Dale walked out into the beaten path before the store and stopped in surprise when he saw the rider come over the last rise. It was Ford.

Knowing his brother thoroughly he was certain that something important must have happened to force Ford into taking a long horseback ride. Ford considered his personal comfort above all else, and sentiment would never have sent him into these hills.

Dale walked out to meet him and Ford halted the horse, easing his cramped muscles in the saddle.

"Get down," Dale invited. "You're just in time to eat."

"Eating can wait." Ford seemed to be laboring under an inner excitement which whipped away his usual cynical air. "You've certainly played hell now."

"What have I done?"

"You've scared King. I never believed it was possible to scare him into anything, but you have. You and that she-wolf Clara."

"What are you talking about?"

Ford swung down heavily. "Damn the first man who thought up the idea of riding a horse. My backbone feels like it's been shortened three inches."

"You've been sitting in that chair at the poker table too long."

"Every man to his last." Ford loosened the knot in the split reins and let the animal loose to graze.

"What's this I'm supposed to have done?"

Ford said, "It isn't all you. That scheming female probably had more to do with it than you did, although the pressure you've been putting on King helped. Anyhow, he's rounding up every head of stock on the ranch—feeders, she stuff, calves."

"Pushing them back from the timber so my

men can't raid them as easily. I watched them this morning."

"If that was all do you think I'd have ridden clear up here? He's getting set to pull out."

"Pull out?" The idea had not occurred to Dale that King would ever pull out. "You're crazy."

"It's King that's crazy, and it's that woman who's got him crazy. Oh, I have to hand it to Clara. She played him against Les until she got Les killed. Then she tells him that you are going to win in the long run and that all she has to do is wait and marry you."

"I don't believe she said a thing like that."

"You don't believe because you don't want to believe." Ford's voice lacked its usual moderation and rose a little shrilly. "Don't think I'm inventing this. I made it a point to listen to them last night. She laid it right out on the line finally. She said that she'd marry him, but only if he sold out the ranch and took her clear away from this valley. He said he couldn't sell it, that he only had a lifetime interest, that at his death it came to you and me."

Dale was staring at the grazing horse, trying to picture the scene in his mind. His impulse was to reject Ford's words, but he could see the picture nevertheless: King and the girl perhaps beside the hotel desk, Ford in the corridor above, listening as he himself had once listened.

The very thought of the whole thing made Dale

a little sick. Clara and King. He'd have to stop that. King would agree to anything to get her, but once he had her he'd break her to his will as he had broken everyone he had ever come into contact with.

"But she showed him the way," Ford went on. "She said that no one could keep him from selling the cattle, and that after all the ranch without the cattle was like you said in the street, just a few buildings and three deeded sections of land. She said you and I could have the buildings and the land. With the money they got from the cattle he and she could live like a real king and queen."

Ford turned and spat as if in an effort to get the sour taste of the words out of his mouth.

"At first King wouldn't listen. So she said it was his last chance. Either he agreed to take her away from the valley or she'd marry you."

Dale winced.

"When she said that you should have heard him. He really blew his top. He's got it bad, real bad. I never saw King go for women much before, but I guess that's the worst kind. When they begin to get young ideas at their age they really fall off the roof. He finally agreed, so they kissed and everything was lovely."

He did not seem to see Dale's strained face.

"I won't let her do it."

"I'm afraid you just can't stop her," Ford said.

Dale turned on him angrily. "Oh yes I can. He

can round up those cattle from hell to breakfast, but he can't sell them without getting them out of the valley, right?"

His brother nodded slowly. "That's right."

"So how is he going to get them out? Lucy Colton has already told him never to drive over her ranch again. She means it, and if you think King has a tough crew, just watch that crazy Russian and his men. The only other way out is up this canyon, and we'd cut them to pieces if they tried that."

Ford shook his head. "I wish I was as sure as you are. You don't know it, but one of the Thunderhead crew is kind of working for me. I pay him any time he has a little information he thinks I can use."

Dale gaped at his brother. It was, he thought, almost impossible that they had the same mother. Ford had gotten nothing of the mother's softness and gentleness. He was as hard as a piece of shining glass, and as brittle. The news that his brother, Les, had been murdered had not affected him visibly, even when it was plain that he shared Dale's suspicion that King had killed his own son. Now he readily admitted that he kept a paid spy to watch his father's movements.

"Tell me," Dale asked suddenly. "Do you think King himself killed Les?"

His brother showed surprise at the shift in

155

conversation. "What makes you ask that? What difference does it make?"

"That first night in the saloon, you made a remark about knowing who killed Les."

"All right, I did."

"And you thought it was King."

Ford took time to answer. "It was an idea I had." He said this slowly. "I thought if I ever needed a hold on him I'd use that."

Dale said shortly, "All right. Come on and eat. Then we'll ride."

"Ride?" Ford groaned. "I've ridden enough today to last me a lifetime. Where are we going?"

"Back to Climax. I'm going to talk to Clara. I'm going to tell her that she can't marry King. Even if everything you say about her is the truth I still think I can convince her. I'll explain that no matter what King wants to do he can't get those cows out of this valley alive."

CHAPTER THIRTEEN

It was almost three o'clock in the morning when they came down out of Loud Canyon, across the bridge and into Climax. Even the lights in the Palace Saloon were out, and Dale thought, as he pulled his horse up before the hotel and stepped down, that the nightly poker game had probably ended early because Ford had not been there to keep it going.

They had not spoken a dozen words during the long ride. Ford was apparently too occupied with his saddle sores to give much attention to anything else, and Dale's bitter thoughts had not been such that he wanted to share them.

He felt as if his whole world was coming to an end. He had lived for two things only: to get the ranch which was rightfully his, then to marry Clara. It was ironic, he thought as he fastened the horse and moved on up the hotel steps, pushing open the door and stepping into the dark lobby, that he had known Clara nearly his full life and not really noticed her until his return.

Ford followed him into the lobby. Dale would much rather not have his brother along, but he understood that in certain ways Ford's interest was as deep as his own.

He struck a light and in its tiny flame found a

bracket lamp on the wall at the foot of the stairs and lit it.

"Which is Clara's room?"

Ford pointed. "The one at the head of the staircase, on the right."

Dale climbed the steps, making no effort to be quiet, and the thump of Ford's boots on the hollow treads sounded like thunder in his ears. He paused to light the bracketed lamp in the upper hall, then knocked on her door.

Clara's voice reached him, small, uncertain, a little frightened, and again he knew the wave of protective feeling which had not been quenched even by Ford's account of what she had said to King.

"It's Dale, Clara." His tone was soft. "Nothing to be frightened of, but I have to talk to you."

He heard her move inside. He heard her slide the bolt on the door, then she pulled it open.

Her face was flushed with sleep, her eyes very deep and dark, with only a hint of greenness. She wore a loose wrapper over her full-length night gown.

"Dale. What's happened?" She saw Ford across his shoulder and her eyes widened.

"Do you want to come downstairs and talk?"

She said slowly, "What's there to talk about?"

"Several things. I'm sorry about the hour, but it couldn't be helped."

"I don't know why we can't talk here."

He took a slow, deep breath. "I hear you're going to marry King."

Again her eyes went across his shoulder to Ford in the background. "You told him," she murmured accusingly. "I had a hunch you were listening last night."

Ford had recovered his composure. "Was there something you didn't want repeated?" The usual mockery was back in his voice.

"No." She was a full match for him, perfectly capable of holding up her end. "There's no reason for anyone not to know. I am going to marry King."

Dale could not say that he had not expected this after Ford's revelations to him. But hearing it from her still came as a jolt. She looked so soft, so feminine with her red hair curling airily about the white shoulders of her gown, so small without her shoes to give her stature.

He reached out and closed his big hands over those shoulders, pulling her against him, suddenly unconscious of the brother who stood behind him.

"Listen to me, Clara. You've lost your perspective. Les's death did something to you. You can't marry King."

She raised her small hands, pressing them against his chest. Now she pushed, trying to free herself.

He let her go reluctantly and she looked at him

159

with level eyes, saying in a controlled voice, "I wish this hadn't happened, Dale. Honestly I do. I think I've come closer to loving you than any man I have ever known. But I have to be practical."

He told her wildly, "Who wants to be practical?" and tried once more to draw her into his arms. But as if she sensed his intent, she took another step backward into her room.

"Listen to me." There was a metallic note in her voice which held his attention. "I've never tried to fool you, have I? I want to get away from this town, this valley. You can't understand this. You've been away, and you came back, but you aren't a woman. You don't know what this country does to a woman."

He said gently, "And you don't know what King Parson can do to a woman. I do. I've seen it."

"That doesn't worry me. I can handle King. All we want is to be let alone. I'll tell you something, Dale. If things had been different I could have loved you."

He said steadily, and it took effort, "Listen to me a minute. You think King is going to sell the cows off Thunderhead. You think you and he will take the money and go a long way away from this valley. I rode in to tell you that you are wrong, to try to warn you in time. King is not going to drive one cow off Thunderhead. There are only

160

two ways he can get stock to the railroad; one is across the Colton range, south. He won't go that way. Lucy Colton and her crew are there waiting. The other way, the tougher way, is north through Squaw Canyon into Wyoming. He isn't going that way either, because I have a hundred armed men just waiting for him to try. I can't blame you for trying, Clara, but I can try to stop you, from throwing your life away on something entirely hopeless."

She was watching him. Suddenly she laughed. "Dale," her voice was not unkind. "Poor Dale. That's the difference between you and King. You figure things out the way you think they have to be, and then you say that anything else is impossible. I don't want you hurt. I shouldn't say this, but maybe I owe you the warning. King knows as well as you the problems he faces, and he has figured out a way. Doesn't it occur to you that he might hire extra men, that he might fight his way through to the railroad?"

Dale could think of nothing to say.

She told him quietly, "I don't think there is anything else to talk about."

He realized then that nothing he had said was of any avail. He could continue to argue but he knew with sudden certainty that it was all futile.

His voice was quiet, but there was a note of finality in it. "All right, Clara. If that's the way you want it."

Her answer was almost a cry. "Dale, it isn't the way I want it, but it's the way it is."

He turned then and found himself facing Ford. He had forgotten that his brother was there.

"Let's go."

They did not blow out the hall light. They did not look back. They did not know that the girl stood in the open doorway watching them until they disappeared from sight, that she was still there when she heard the outer door slam, and that she was crying.

Ford stopped on the sidewalk and his voice was oddly embarrassed when he spoke. "I'm sorry, Dale."

His older brother said, "For what?"

"For you. You believed in her as I have never believed in anything in this world. Nothing anyone could say would change your belief. You had to have it from her."

"Forget it."

"She's very confident. Do you suppose King has a way to get the cattle out of the valley after all?"

"Impossible."

"Is it? Think a minute. Maybe he's made a deal with Lucy Colton."

"Absurd. Lucy wouldn't make a deal with King in a million years. I know her."

"Do you? Suppose King went to her and said he was pulling out. Suppose he said he was stripping

Thunderhead of cattle, that all he wanted was a final passage for his herd through her ranch. Think what it would mean to her. You and I have no cows to throw on the range. There would be nothing to keep her from driving part of her herd up through Loud Canyon and scattering them across the range. She'd like that."

Dale was stubborn. "I tell you she wouldn't do it. Even for that she wouldn't do a thing that would help King Parson."

"You thought you knew Clara too."

Dale glared at him, the heat of anger climbing through him. "Let me alone unless you want to get hurt."

Ford said, "I don't want to get hurt, either by you or by King. You can sit up in that canyon and wait for him to try to drive through the hills if you want to. Me, I intend to find out what is going on." He turned, got his horse and headed for the livery.

The eastern sky was full light now. In half an hour the sun would clear the hills and it would be day. Dale stood for a long minute looking after his brother. Ford's words haunted him. Clara had been so very confident that King had a way out. Was Ford right? Had Lucy made a deal to let King drive to the railroad? It was not a solution that would have occurred to Dale, he admitted to himself. But then, his mind did not operate in the devious patterns followed by Ford.

And Ford was very like King in many ways. It certainly might have occurred to King. Yet he kept remembering Lucy's hatred. He would gamble his life that she would not deviate from her path one inch for anyone. Whatever else she was, she was strong-minded, and she was honest even in her hate.

Dale got his horse and rode slowly from the town. After he emerged from Loud Canyon he swung out of the road and skirted the line of timber along the bench. It took an hour longer than if he had stayed in the trail, but he had no desire to encounter any of the Thunderhead crew that morning. All he saw during the trip was an occasional steer apparently missed in King's sweeping roundup. And the knowledge that they had actually grouped the bulk of the cattle near the home ranch only aggravated his worry.

He reached the mouth of Squaw Canyon finally and turned his horse into it, welcoming the shade beneath the sharp walls after the heat of the morning sun. He was bone-tired, washed out from both exertion and from the emotional scene with Clara.

Twice he was tempted to turn into the safety of a side canyon and lie down to sleep. But he knew that his crew would be waiting, restless against his return, and he pressed on, riding up the twisting trail to reach the store in midafternoon.

Most of the men in his crew were lounging

on the store porch and they watched silently as he rode in. He stepped down, motioning one of the men to take his horse. Then he crossed to the steps where Boyer and Pops Jordan squatted in the patch of shade cast by the roof peak.

"What did you find out?" It was Boyer.

"Looks like King's pulling out."

"Out?" Surprise ran through the group. They could not have been more amazed if he had told them that the rock face of Thunderhead mountain had suddenly fallen into dust. "What do you mean, pulling out?"

"He's stripping the range of every head of stock he can gather. He intends to drive to the railroad, sell them all and get out of the country."

"Why?" Boyer's voice showed its incredulity. "We haven't scared him that bad yet."

Dale hesitated, still reluctant to drag Clara's name into any general discussion. But he needed these men and they would only continue to ride with him as long as they trusted him and fully understood what was happening.

"He wants to get married," Dale said. "And the woman he wants won't marry him if he stays at Thunderhead."

They considered this, each man turning over the news, making his own appraisal. It was Boyer who asked, "How does he plan to get out of the valley? The Coltons wouldn't let him through to the south last year."

"And I don't think they will now. He drove up Squaw Canyon last year."

"We weren't camped here then."

"No," Dale said, and his words were heavy with meaning. "We weren't camped here then."

Suddenly Boyer chuckled as if the idea amused him more than anything had in a long time. "Kind of looks like we've been wasting time, gathering critters and driving them up here. Looks like King is maybe fixing to save us the trouble."

"Maybe." Dale walked over to the whiskey barrel at the corner of the porch and drew a small drink. "But there's talk that King has a plan. Maybe he's going to hire a lot more men and punch his way through."

"Maybe. It will take a lot."

A murmur ran through the group and he turned to look at them. Two weeks before these men had been scattered through the hills, each depending on his own strength, his own resources to keep himself alive. But in this short time they had been welded into a crew, sensing the strength of concerted effort, each taking pride in being a member of a group. He was abruptly proud of them, of the steady way they met his glance, of the amused eagerness with which they faced the possibility of an all-out fight with Thunderhead. Alone not one of them had ever dared to stand up to the big ranch. Now they were contemptuous of it.

He said, "There's not much we can do except wait, but let's double the guards and send a few men down to watch the trail and the grass. We don't want to be caught unprepared."

Boyer nodded.

"I'm going to get some sleep." Dale walked to the bunkhouse, got a blanket and carried it back under a tree at the edge of the clearing.

It was full dark when he woke, and he could see the men clustered around the fire beyond the log house. He rose, stiff from the long ride, and moved in to find that the cook had left a pot of beans and a chunk of meat warming for him.

He ate standing beside the stove, then poured himself coffee from the blackened pot. He was half through the coffee when he heard horses coming up the canyon. He stepped outside, glancing at his watch as he did so, and was surprised that it was after midnight.

The men at the fire had risen and several were holding rifles. This, he thought, was an alert bunch, as wary of danger as any animal.

The horses came on, crossed the last rise, and in the moonlight he saw there were two men.

He walked forward as they came to the fire, and recognized one of his own men. The second rider was Old Coke.

He dropped the cup, going quickly to help the old cook from his saddle, to hear the rider say, "I

167

met him coming up the canyon. He said he had to talk to Bronco in a hurry."

Dale turned again to Coke. The old man was in bad shape, and he wheezed as he lifted his bulk to the ground. There was a savage bruise on one cheek and dried blood matted his hair beneath the edge of his broken hat.

"Coke, what happened to you?"

"It ain't me," said Coke. He was still wheezing a little. "It's Ford. He's dead. They killed him."

CHAPTER FOURTEEN

Coke sounded on the verge of collapse, but he stayed on his feet and asked hoarsely, "Is there any drinking liquor in this place?"

Dale nodded to one of the watching men. He himself ran to the store porch, filling a tin cup so full that the liquor slopped over as he carried it across the rough ground.

The old man seized it with both hands. Even then Dale had to steady it to keep him from sloshing it down his shirt front. Not until the cup was empty did Coke settle back with a sigh.

"Man, another mile and I'd never have made her."

"Let's look at that head," Dale suggested.

"Head's all right. Ain't the first time she's been split a bit. Let me tell you about Ford."

"We're waiting. Take your time."

The old man breathed deeply. It was as if he savored the details of the story and wanted to get the most out of the telling.

"It was right after noon when he rode into the ranch yard. I'd seen him coming but I didn't think nothing about it. The crew has been busy as beavers the last two days, gathering the herd." His eyes had brightened a little.

"Could I have some more of that there whiskey?"

One of the crew went to refill the cup.

"I was just bussing up the dishes." The old man's voice was stronger. "When he rode up he says, 'You got an extra cup, Coke?' Sounded just like he did when he was a kid. I got him the coffee and he drank it scalding like. 'Where's King,' he says.

"I said he'd gone up to the main house with Mark Jacoby, and after he finished his coffee Ford started up there. I was plumb curious, but I didn't want nobody to know I was even interested. King's been as touchy as a shedding rattler the last few days, so I cut around the blacksmith shed to the corral and around it to that swale that runs up to the back of the house.

"By the time I got to the corner King and Mark Jacoby had come out on the porch and down the steps and they were standing with their backs to me, facing Ford, and they were already arguing."

"Did you hear what was said?" Dale asked sharply.

"Mostly, I guess. Ford was mad. You can always tell when he's mad by the quiet way he talks. He said he knew King was rounding up the herd. He said he'd told you but that you weren't doing anything about it, just sitting up here in this canyon waiting for King to drive the cows up to you."

"What did King say?"

"He tried to laugh. He said Ford was plumb out of his head to think King would even think of leaving Thunderhead. Ford cut him short. Ford said he'd talked to Clara Austin and he knew the full story, and that King could make a damn fool of himself about the little witch if he wanted to.

"That's when King hit him. He knocked him a good six feet backward, and Ford lit sitting down, holding his jaw and staring up at King. And if I ever see murder in a man's eye I seen it in Ford's then.

"He took his time getting up. He even dusted off the seat of his pants. Then he stood there looking at King. 'You'll be sorry for that,' he says. I could just barely hear him. 'I know you killed Les because of that fool girl, and I wasn't going to do anything about it, but I am now. I'm going to kill you.'

"He went for his gun as he talked, and Ford is pretty fast. Faster than King ever was, and I've seen King draw a gun a lot of times. Ford would have beat him. I guess King knew that. He never even made a move for his gun.

"It was Mark Jacoby who drew, and he's as fast as anyone I ever saw. He put three bullets into Ford before Ford even got his gun clear. Then he walked over and stood over him.

" 'You fool,' Jacoby said, 'It was me killed Les,

not King.' And then he shot Ford in the head, just to make certain."

There wasn't a sound from the listening men. Finally Dale said slowly, his voice tight with shock and outrage. "And what happened to you?"

"Me?" The old man had apparently forgotten his cracked head. "Oh, that was my own fault. If I'd stayed quiet I don't think they'd ever have seen me. They were talking about carting Ford back and burying him before the rest of the crew got in from the herd. I figured I'd better get out of there, so I twisted around and turned my ankle on a stone and fell down.

"They heard me and Mark was around the corner like a cat. I'd got to my hands and knees and he kicked me here. I went flat, and then they hauled me up and I sure figured he was going to shoot me right then. Instead he cracked me along the side of my head with his gun barrel and I went out."

"How'd you get away?"

The old man chuckled to himself. "Guess they just didn't know how hard my head is. I came to and they were up beside the rock, planting Ford. His horse was out in front of the house and I figured that if I wanted to live I'd best get out of there.

"I climbed aboard and walked him, keeping the house between us until I got to the lane, then I hi-tailed. There wasn't another horse saddled and I figured they'd never get me. I headed right across the range for the brush, then worked my way down to this canyon."

"So it was Jacoby who killed Les." Somehow the knowledge eased things a little for Dale. He could understand King killing a man in a fight, or even bushwhacking him. But it had been hard to believe that even his stepfather would ride up beside his own son, put a gun to the back of his head and pull the trigger.

"Yes, the murdering bastard's got no feelings," growled Coke. "Ever since he came to the ranch things have been going from bad to worse. Lord knows, King didn't need no one to think up devilment, but somehow the two of them offset each other. What one wouldn't think of the other did. Jacoby thinks King's the best in the world. He'd do anything for him, and I guess when Les and his Dad had trouble Jacoby just stepped in and settled it."

Dale said, "What about this roundup?"

"Kin I have another drink?"

"After I've fixed that head. But first tell me, do you know what King is aiming to do?"

The old cook shook his head. "The crew's talked some. They're curious, but he ain't told no one unless it's Jacoby, and Jacoby never says a word."

"Is he hiring extra men?"

The cook shook his head. "I ain't seen none,

but he could have some riders who ain't come back to the ranch. The boys have been riding from morning till night."

"All right, let's have a look at you." Dale wheeled around and told one of the men to get a bucket of hot water and another cup of whiskey.

Nursing the whiskey between his twisted hands, Old Coke sat quiet while Dale washed the caked blood from the shaggy hair, exposing the broken skin above the left temple. The gun barrel had raised a long welt the size of Dale's thumb on the side of Coke's skull, but as far as Dale could tell the bone had not been shattered.

"Lucky for you that you've got a hard head."

Coke grinned as if it were a compliment. "Always did have, Bronco. And the whiskey I've drunk makes it kind of insensible you might say. I don't feel things like other people do."

He raised the tin cup, drained it and held it out for more. Dale was about to refuse, then changed his mind. Coke must be well over seventy. He had taken enough of a beating to have killed an ordinary man, and then had ridden a good twenty-five miles.

"Give it to him. Maybe he'll sleep."

Coke slept, but Dale did not. The puzzle of what King Parson planned to do haunted him like a nagging dream. Could Ford possibly be right? Would Lucy Colton make a deal with King to let his herd cross her ranch, glad of the chance to be rid of Thunderhead for all time?

With King gone, and the cattle gone, where would Dale be? Not much better off than the hill ranchers who made up his crew. Not as well, in fact, for they had a few cows to start with, while he had none. He would not even have title to the home place until King died, and if King merely disappeared he might never gain a clear title to it.

He rode at daylight. He roused Boyer and talked to him for twenty minutes, warning him to keep the men alert and that if King tried to drive through the canyon before Dale returned, to let him come on. Men were to be posted on the canyon sides and they were to wait until the drag was already in the hills before they cut down on the crew.

He dropped out of the canyon on a fresh horse and angled across the grass toward Thunderhead, watchful for any of his stepfather's men.

He had no real idea of what he intended to do, but the conviction was growing in his mind that this would not end until he had killed King or had been killed by him. Les was gone. So was Ford. The fact that Mark Jacoby had pulled the triggers made small difference. King Parson had, by his actions, killed both of them.

Dale was no hypocrite. He had had small liking for Les, and little respect for Ford, and he knew that if the positions had been reversed neither of his brothers would have raised a finger to avenge his death.

He was not actually thinking of vengeance then, when he made his decision that King must die. Rather, it was the knowledge that as long as the man lived he would continue to bring pain and grief to everyone, including Clara.

His thinking about the girl was mixed. He could not help blaming her, but also he had spent enough of his life under the domination of King Parson to realize that his stepfather was a hard man to stand against. If the only way to protect Clara was to kill King, then King must die.

He was within five miles of the ranch and had seen no one when he first spotted the dust. It was a great enveloping cloud and it rose not in the direction of the ranch but out on the trail toward Climax, and he was seized with a sudden suspicion. Yet King might still be at Thunderhead, so he headed for the huge rock face rising out of the bench, the landmark that could be seen for miles.

As he approached the yard he slowed his pace, watchful now for signs of life. There were none. No smoke rose from the cook house chimney, nothing moved in any of the smaller buildings and the horse corral was empty.

He rode in, still cautious, but there was no one

there. Stepping from the saddle, he went into the bunkhouse. The blankets were gone from the bunks and no spare clothes hung from the row of pegs.

He came again into the sunlight, considering, then turned toward the main house. As soon as he stepped inside he knew that King Parson was gone for good.

King had never been a tidy man and the house looked as if it had been struck by a cyclone. Drawers had been pulled out and still gaped open. Papers, receipted bills, memorabilia of all kinds lay scattered across the floor.

Dale climbed to his mother's room. Only here was there any degree of order. It was apparent that King had cared nothing for those things which his dead wife had treasured through her years.

Dale turned away. It was like walking through an abandoned graveyard. He came down the steps, welcoming the warm glare of the afternoon sun and stood for a moment visualizing the yard as it might be.

King had run a womanless ranch, as the saying went, and his lack of orderliness showed itself here as it had within the house. Broken wagon equipment had been carelessly pushed out of the way. The cook shack roof had been patched with old tin cans flattened for the purpose. It looked, thought Dale, like a rawhider's outfit, not the most powerful ranch in the valley.

He moved back to where he had left his horse beside the corral fence, swung up and rode slowly out along the lane toward the distant road.

He found the bed ground where the herd had been held for at least two days, but the hoof marks as they turned toward Climax were now twenty-four hours old, and there were no fresh droppings. Apparently, then, the movement had not begun this day, but on the preceding afternoon, probably shortly after Ford's death.

And they were moving rapidly. The dust cloud far to the south was only a thin haze kicked up by the drag. The main herd would by now be through Loud Canyon, already through Climax, and spilling onto Colton range.

Dale wondered what was happening there. Had Lucy actually made her deal for this passage or was King Parson trying to bull his way through, figuring that he would have less trouble with the Colton crew than trying to drive up the narrow twisting Squaw Canyon trail against the opposition of the hill ranchers Dale had organized to guard it?

His impulse was to swing that way, to tell his waiting men what had happened, to take them racing after the cattle. But two things kept him from riding back to the canyon. It would take him all night, probably until noon tomorrow, to make the circuit and ride with his men into Climax. By following the road he could reach Loud Canyon shortly after sundown.

The other reason was that he did not want to start a three-way battle if it could be avoided, his men on one side against Thunderhead and the IC together. Both King's and Lucy Colton's crews were trained gunfighters, paid extra wages for just that reason.

Dale hesitated to send his small ranchers against them, to perhaps get twenty men killed. It was one thing to ask them to make a stand in Squaw Canyon where the terrain favored them, where each rider knew every foot of the rough ground and where he could snipe at the trail drivers from the protection of the rocks and trees. It was quite another to ask them to ride into the open, onto Colton range where they had no legal right to be, and to face the murderous fire of the two ruthless crews.

He headed for town. He meant to find out what had happened at the south end of the valley. If Lucy had given Thunderhead free passage he knew that he was licked. He could not catch the herd in time to get it back into the hills where he could hold it in spite of the law.

Thunderhead would be through, a matter of history. This was what hurt him most—not the idea of personal loss but the passing of the ranch.

The ranch to him had never been an impersonal thing. It was a living, breathing entity as important as any person, as loved as any woman. He spurred his horse into a hard run.

CHAPTER FIFTEEN

Dale came down through Loud Canyon fast, but hardly faster than King Parson was pushing the cattle. It was obvious that King had driven all night, obvious that his men had kept relentless pressure on the animals, probably urged on by fear that Dale and his hill men might strike them from behind.

Climax lay as it had for a long time, quiet in the late evening. He reined his horse up before the Palace Saloon, draped the lines over the hitch rail and walked into the long room. He stepped through the doors and the conversation at the bar died as if on signal.

He walked forward to the bar, knowing that the sudden tension would hold until he spoke.

The bartender approached slowly as if reluctant to serve his latest customer and Dale said, "How long since the last of the Thunderhead herd went through?"

The bartender shrugged. "A couple of hours."

Dale had his drink and stepped outside. The lights of the hotel lobby attracted him, but he hesitated before turning toward them. He was ravenously hungry, not having eaten through the whole day.

He came in to find that the dining room had

not yet been cleared although there were no late diners visible. He crossed and pushed open the kitchen door, having noted from the used plates at the long table that at least a dozen people had eaten.

Clara was alone at the sink washing dishes. She did not hear him, did not turn until he spoke, and he stood for a long silent minute watching her.

"You must have had a crowd, feeding King and his men."

She turned then, surprise not unmixed with fear leaping into her eyes.

"Dale. What are you doing here?"

He said, "I came to get something to eat, or do you only feed Thunderhead?"

She flushed, but failed to answer. She cleared one side of the kitchen table, placed silver, a plate and a cup, and motioned him to sit down.

He eased his tired body into the chair, watched while she ladled stew onto the plate and filled his coffee cup.

"I'm curious. Did King make a deal with Lucy Colton to drive across her ranch? Or is he going to try to bull his way through?"

She took a long moment to answer. "He isn't going to bull through."

A sharp pang of disappointment hit Dale. He had expected more from Lucy Colton. He did not know why it was important to his peace of mind that Lucy stick to her announced intent, but it was.

"Dale." Clara was standing on the far side of the table, her arms bare to the elbows, firmly rounded, with a few freckles showing upon their backs. "What are you going to do?"

His impulse was to say in bitterness, "What can I do? My men are up in the canyon, too far away to be of any use this night. And even if they weren't, the fighting would begin as soon as I led them onto Colton range, and we would have to battle both crews."

Instead he said, "We'll wait and see."

"There's been trouble enough. Let them go without any more fighting. Please. Let them go and I'll promise to make King send you back the deeds to Thunderhead."

He could have said, "Thanks for nothing." He ate on in silence.

Clara's voice was small. "You hate me, don't you?"

Strangely he did not hate her. That depth of feeling was reserved for his stepfather, although he realized that Clara was probably more responsible for the movement of the herd than was King.

"No," he said. "I'm sorry for you."

"Sorry?" Surprise made her voice almost shrill. "Sorry, Dale? You don't understand what getting away from this town means to me, what it will mean to have enough money for good clothes, money enough to go and see the places I've only read about, to live like a white person instead of a squaw. Why should you be sorry for me?"

"You'll have King."

She said quickly, "I can handle King, never fear."

That, he thought, was her deep mistake. She could handle King now, yes; now while their relationship was new, while King wanted her so badly that he would pay any price to get her.

But that would change, for King's basic nature was not altered. He might make promises now in good faith, but he had never kept any promises during his full life when they did not serve his purpose.

Dale finished his meal and pushed back his chair, rising. "I hope you can handle him. I wish you luck."

"Why, thank you." She was startled. "That's very nice of you, Dale. You are a good person." She came around the corner of the table, almost shyly.

"Dale, would you kiss me good-by?"

He did not want to kiss her. He wanted to slap her, but she was very close now, and he felt the familiar, urgent pull of her animal magnetism. This girl always had had the power to stir him no matter what she did.

He kissed her, trying to make it gentle, a casual

contact of their lips, but she slipped both arms around his neck, clinging fiercely as if she could not bear to let him go.

He reached up, unclasping her hands and pushing her gently away. "The trouble is, Clara, you don't actually know what you do want. And you can't have everything in this life."

He turned then and left the room, moving slowly to his horse, still undecided on the course he should follow. Finally he mounted and rode out of town, heading south.

Along the trail he saw a dozen animals in the moonlight, all bearing the Thunderhead brand, animals that had played out under the harsh drive and been left behind.

He had journeyed six miles when he heard the drum of hoofs. He had been riding slowly and now he pulled out of the trail, around a burst of rocks upthrust like a sentinel from the valley floor.

The moon almost directly overhead turned everything around him into liquid silver, almost as sharp as daylight, and he watched as they came toward him.

The rider in front was a good quarter of a mile ahead of the others, and it was obvious that they were in pursuit. Then Dale swore softly. The leading rider was a woman, Lucy Colton, and one of the men riding after her was Sarcoff.

The girl, Dale realized, was out-distancing

them. Being lighter, her horse was running easily while the others labored. He let her pass him, then with a careful rifle's shot he killed Sarcoff's horse.

The big man turned over completely in the air and lit on his back. The rider with him hauled up, craning toward the rocks from which the shot had come, then reared around and raked his horse in a desperate plunge to get out of range.

The girl had stopped a thousand yards beyond Dale and swung her horse, sitting a little uncertainly, for the moment not recognizing him.

He paid no attention to her. He rode out onto the trail, saw Sarcoff struggle upward to his hands and knees, and thought that the man must be indestructible. That fall would have killed the average man.

The Russian came to his feet, recognizing Dale, and the sound which welled from his throat was a roar of anger. His hand dropped to his gun.

Dale's rifle steadied. "Don't try it."

Either the man did not hear him or he was so shaken by his fall and by the sudden appearance of Dale that he paid no attention. His gun came up. Its first heavy bullet cut a notch in Dale's hat brim.

Dale did not hurry. His rifle leveled and he shot the Russian directly between the eyes.

For an instant it seemed to him that he must have missed. Sarcoff remained standing his feet planted wide apart, his gun arm raised. Then the arm fell and he toppled forward onto his face.

Behind him Dale heard Lucy's horse as she rode back to his side. She sat for a long moment, unmoving, gazing down at her dead foreman. Then she turned and he saw the relief in her eyes. "Thank you."

He said, "You'd have been all right. You were outrunning them."

She shook her head. "No, I wouldn't. They'd have come into Climax after me, and no one there would have stood against Sarcoff."

He said, "Why were they chasing you?"

She was surprised. "Don't you know what has happened?"

"How could I?"

"But you were following King."

"I know he is driving across your range. I thought he had your permission."

Her head came up. "My permission? I'd never give King permission to cross the IC."

"Then how?"

"Sarcoff and the crew sold out. I don't know when the deal was made. We'd just completed our own roundup yesterday, and were going to cut out a shipping herd when King rode in with two men. I ordered him off the place and he laughed at me. He said maybe I'd better talk to Sarcoff.

"I called Sarcoff over and told him to run King out, and Sarcoff laughed, too. Vince was there. He started to draw on Sarcoff and they killed him." Her voice broke a little. "They shot him down from both sides."

Dale stared at her incredulously.

"Then they started running the Thunderhead brand on all my cattle."

This was almost past belief. "They stole your stock?"

She said in deep bitterness, "They are cleaning all the cows out of the valley. King isn't coming back. None of them are coming back. I don't know what he's paying Sarcoff and my crew, but it must be a huge slice, otherwise they wouldn't have changed sides."

Dale shook his head slowly. "This doesn't make very good sense."

Her voice was tight. "It makes good sense as far as King Parson is concerned. I've got over ten thousand head. He has almost the same. Say they average out at ten dollars a head, she stock and calves thrown in. That comes to nearly a quarter of a million dollars."

"He'll never get away with it," Dale said grimly.

"Maybe. The deal was that they forced me to sign a bill of sale, then they took me back to the ranch and Sarcoff and that other man stayed to guard me while King and the two crews started to re-work my herd. I slipped out tonight while they were eating, grabbed a horse and headed for Climax."

"Why? You said there was no help there for you."

She met his eyes steadily. "I wasn't going to stop in Climax. I was going there to ask where to find you."

He experienced a sudden impulse to laugh, not from humor but from irony that she should be forced to turn to him for help. Then the laughter died.

"We'll have to get out of here." She was speaking quickly. "The man with Sarcoff—the one who got away—will alert King and they'll start hunting me. King can't leave me free. If I were to contact the cattle buyers he'd never collect for the herd."

Dale nodded, his features gray and taciturn. "How far ahead is King?"

"Not far. The drag is less than two miles. They're driving it slow now to mix with my herd."

He said suddenly, "Ride back to Squaw Valley," Dale directed. "You can get a fresh horse at the livery. Get hold of Clem Boyer. Tell him to bring every man he can get his hands on. I'm going to stampede that herd when they hit that rough stretch beyond your ranch."

Lucy shook her head. "I'd never make it in

time. They'll be through the rocks and into the pass. Once they reach the crest we'd have no chance to stop them. They've got fifty men or better in the combined crews. Ten of them could hold us at the pass while the others drove on to the railroad."

"They aren't going to make the pass." Dale's voice was grim, his eyes like splinters of hard steel.

"Who's going to stop them?" Lucy demanded.

"I am."

She gasped. "But how?"

"Stampede. Scatter them clear across the range and into the bench brush. It will take weeks to round them up again. By that time I'll have every man in the hills riding at my back."

"I'm going with you," Lucy declared. "Two of us can work twice as quickly as one."

"No. You go after my men."

A sudden fierce note came into her voice. "I'm not going. Whose cows are they stealing? Whose brother was just murdered? All I want is to get King Parson in my rifle sights. I don't care what happens after that."

Dale abruptly held up his hand. The steady drum of running horses was carried to them on the wings of the night wind.

"We haven't much time." He did not argue with her further. She probably would never make Climax now anyhow. Certainly she would not make it to Squaw Canyon where his men were stationed.

"Come on, let's get out of here." He swung directly west, around the rock burst which had served him as shelter, and headed for the dark line the timber made along the hills three miles away.

Lucy pulled in after him and they sent their horses across the foot-high grass at a pitching run.

There was no cover. The land around them rolled like a carpet over an uneven floor and, aside from the occasional upthrusts of rock chimneys, there was nothing high enough to hide a man and a horse.

Behind them they heard a sudden high-pitched yell and knew they had been discovered. Dale twisted in the saddle and saw a dozen riders spill out of the trail, cutting across the valley in their wake.

Certainly King Parson was taking no further chance of the girl's escape, and he thought grimly of the desperation in which King must now be riding. If she won free, if she somehow got in touch with the cattle buyers at the railroad before he had been paid off, all of King's plans would be destroyed.

He glanced at the girl riding easily at his side. Her horse should be fresher than his, for he had been riding it all day. True, it had rested in

Climax, and he had not pushed the animal, but still it had packed his hundred and eighty-five pounds for a long time. He could only hope their pursuers were in no better shape, that they were still riding the same horses with which they had worked the cattle during the better part of the day.

Looking back, it was hard to tell whether or not King's rawhiders were closing ground. The moonlight showed them plainly, but it gave the scene an eerie, unreal quality, making it difficult to judge distance.

The timber loomed measurably closer. They had covered perhaps half the way there when a rifle flashed behind them. Dale did not try to return the fire. Only a lucky shot could possibly find a mark at this distance and he had no ammunition to waste.

The men behind them were firing regularly now, as if in a frantic effort to halt them before they reached the shelter of the trees. But they made it. They slowed to a dangerous walk as the bench steepened and they climbed upward. Then the darkness of the timber closed down around them.

Dale's horse wanted to stop but he spurred it on. They pushed first through the lower brush and then into the pole pine. These at places grew so thickly that it was an effective fence, around which they were forced to circle. Very little light came through the interlocking branches, and the girl rode as close as she could, as if afraid they would be separated.

Below they could hear the crash of horses and the curses of the riders who forged after them. The grade steepened and Dale swung left, eventually finding a deer trail, which slanted up at an almost impossible angle, then dropped over a sharp ridge, taking them down into a canyon where the trail turned upstream.

Dale halted his laboring horse, sitting quietly, listening to the noise of pursuit. His impulse was to turn up canyon, to seek higher ground as quickly as possible. But there was the possibility that the canyon would box out and that the sides would be too steep to climb. If so they would be trapped. But, even as he hesitated, his choice was made for him. Noises came from downstream, and he realized that some of the pursuers had broken over the ridge below him.

He turned up, urging his horse through the mat of bushes along the creek and came finally to a beaver dam which spread its shallow sheet of water clear across the canyon floor. It made a bog through which he was afraid to attempt to ride.

There was nothing for it but to try the sharp rising face of the canyon wall. It could be climbed on foot, he judged after a careful look. But whether a horse would make the ascent was another question.

He put the horse at it, pawing and struggling, rising in heaving lunges until they came to a slide of loose rock that had cut a fifty-foot wide strip down through the timber.

Dale dismounted and began to lead the unhappy animal across, Lucy following him doggedly. Three times the rocks slipped under his horse's feet and once it lay down on its side, shivering in terror.

Dale got it up somehow. Behind him the girl was having a slightly easier time, but her horse kept plunging at her so that she was constantly in danger of being knocked down.

Suddenly, below them, they heard the low voices and shouts of King Parson's men. A rifle flashed. The bullet struck the rocks a hundred feet above Dale and veered off in a screaming ricochet.

And then he reached the ledge, a hummock of solid earth and rock which had broken the progress of the slide. He led his horse around a shoulder, tied it to a tree which clung with grasping roots to the stone face above them, and came back to reach out for the struggling girl.

He caught her arm, guided her to safety, then brought in her shying horse and led it around the rocky corner now protecting them from bullets.

He came back to the slide then, for Parson's men had left their animals and were trying to climb the canyon side on foot.

CHAPTER SIXTEEN

He heard rather than saw them as he swung around the corner. The girl pressed close to the rock shelf to let him pass. She had drawn her gun, but he shook his head.

"Go back and see if there's a way off this shelf while I hold them. If there is, lead the horses up."

She nodded and was gone. He raised his rifle. He could hear the clatter King's men made in the rocks but, because of the shadow of the trees, he could not see their figures until they reached the far side of the rock slide. There they stopped, and he could hear the mutter of their low voices two hundred feet away.

Then one man bolder than his fellows ventured out onto the slide. Dale had no pity. These men hunting him and the girl were as cruel as a pack of wolves, driven on by nothing more important than a hope of gain.

Dale shot him, and saw the man's arms thrown high into the air and saw him pitch head foremost down the slide, his body turning and twisting, loosening rocks until it became the center of a tiny avalanche.

For a long interval there was silence beyond the slide, then King Parson's clubbing voice struck at him out of the night.

"That you, Dale?"

"It's me." Dale's voice was tight, but there was satisfaction in it.

"You can't get off that ledge."

Dale was uncertain whether they could get off the ledge or not. The rock face above it was nearly vertical. But there were fissures, crevices where a man might get a handhold to help him upward. Certainly he and Lucy could not take their horses up that sheer face, and he had no desire to be afoot in the rough country. Parson and his men could hunt them down at their leisure.

"I think we can. One thing's certain. You can't get across that slide. If you want to try it I'd like nothing better than a shot at you."

Half a dozen bullets suddenly splattered the rock shoulder he was using as a shield. He held his fire, refusing to shoot until he had a clear view of a target.

There was a lull. He heard sounds above him, but a twist in the ledge around which the girl had disappeared hid whatever she was doing.

King's voice came again. "It will be daylight in a couple of hours. We can send half the men down the canyon to a place where they can climb the wall and come back above you."

"Thanks for the warning."

"I'll make a deal. I have no reason to want to hurt either of you. Come across the slide with your hands up and I'll promise nothing will happen to you. We'll take you and the girl back to the Colton ranch and hold you until the cattle are sold. Then we'll take you with us three days into the mountains and turn you loose. By the time you work out and get help we'll be gone."

"Thanks for nothing."

King swore at him. "You never had any sense. All right. Squat there until we come and get you. I'm leaving two men here to see that you don't come back across the slide."

Dale heard them move down through the brush. He even had a moment's glimpse of them at the canyon bottom as they remounted, but it was too far away to risk a shot.

And then he heard the girl behind him, panting a little as if she had been running, and heard her say, "I got the horses to the top."

Dale turned swiftly. Her hair had come loose, trailing down from under the hat around the oval of her face. There was a smudge on her nose and a long scratch across one cheek. Either she had fallen or a branch had raked her face as she passed.

She led the way. The ledge twisted around rock faces at times so narrow that he wondered how she had managed to coax the reluctant horses across. At one place there had been a small slide and she had scooped out the fallen rocks to make a path.

His admiration for her, already high, grew as

they advanced, and finally they reached the crest of the pine-shrouded ridge. There she swayed suddenly, and would have fallen had he not caught her. With a wave of feeling it came to him that she had been pushing herself for the last hour on sheer nerve.

Her eyes were closed. He could not see her face too clearly, for the moon was now well down and the streak of morning had not widened enough in the east to give them much light.

Instinctively, without thinking, he bent his head and pressed his lips gently to hers. He felt her stir in his grasp and she said without opening her eyes, her voice small, weak and far away, "That wasn't necessary."

He knew a surge of quick anger, but in his concern for her put it away almost instantly.

"Are you all right? Can you ride? They've dropped back into the canyon to look for another way up here. I don't know how long it will take them."

"I can ride."

He kept one hand under her arm, escorting her to the tired horses and half lifting her into the saddle. Then he turned along the ridge, searching for an easier descent on the south side.

He found one dropping down a rolling grade into a shallow canyon. He crossed this, climbed the next ridge and found a canyon leading upward toward the distant peaks.

They rode for an hour and a half before he came upon what he sought, a tiny sheltered meadow beside a tiny stream, behind a natural screen of timber. Here he helped Lucy dismount and pulled the saddles from the horses. He hobbled the animals, although both were too weary to have strayed far.

Then he made Lucy a couch with the saddle blankets and saw her curl up and fall instantly asleep. He stood observing her for several minutes, watching the tightness of her face relax, making her look younger and like a sleeping child.

Afterward he moved to a small pool below the trees, stripped and plunged into the icy water. It was so cold that it stung, and he had to grasp an aspen's root to pull himself out. Yet it brought back some of the spring to his flagging muscles. He dressed slowly and had a smoke, his back to a tree, his eyes down the sweep of the valley up which Parson's men must come.

The morning sun was hot and he welcomed the shade. He sat debating. There was coffee and meat in his saddle bags, and some cold biscuits.

He was not sure that it was wise to build a fire but finally decided to risk it, picking his dry sticks carefully so that there would be very little smoke.

The blackened pot from his bed roll on the coals, he waked the girl. He hated to do so, but it was only a matter of time before the men who followed so relentlessly would find the trail they had left in crossing the ridge.

Lucy's eyes were drugged with sleep and she sat up groggily, staring around for a long minute, hardly knowing where she was.

He nodded to the creek. "It's cold, and you'd better hang onto the bank if you want to get out, but it will wake you, believe me."

She rose obediently and disappeared through the screen of trees. He heard the splash and her small gasping cry as she struck the water, and then silence. He listened for a long spell and then straightened.

"Are you all right?"

Her voice came back to him, "All right," the words shaking a little as if her teeth were chattering. A moment later he heard the thrashing as she climbed from the water, and had a small glimpse of her glistening white body as she stepped past a narrow gap in the foliage to retrieve her clothes.

Five minutes later she was at his side, gulping the scalding coffee gratefully, her wet hair tied tightly in a red handkerchief beneath her hat.

"How do you feel?" He was concerned, for they had a long, hard day ahead and she had been close to the breaking point.

"I'm fine. You didn't sleep, did you?"

He shook his head.

"You'd better lie down and let me watch."

"Can't risk it. I figured it would take them a couple of hours to circle back to where they could climb out of that canyon and come along the ridge to cut our trail. That puts them two hours behind us, and we've been here longer than that."

He rose, doused the fire with creek water, then went to saddle the horses. She came to help him.

"Which way are we going?"

He indicated the main ridge and the snow-covered peaks some twenty miles away. "I'm going to swing back toward the hills. I think I know the ground better than King does and I'm certain I know it better than any of the gunfighters in either yours or Thunderhead's crews. If we can get them lost back there by dark we can cut down Shove Hill Canyon and come out close to where the herd is being held. We'll have them scattered over fifty square miles by the time King catches up with us."

Lucy looked at him closely. "You mean you want them to follow us? You mean we're bait?"

"That's the general idea."

She continued to study him. "You love this country, don't you?"

"Don't you?"

"Of course. Why do you think I've fought so hard for the ranch? But I never thought anyone from Thunderhead would think the same way."

He grinned at her. "Lady, there are lots of things you don't really know."

"That's possible." She swung up into the saddle and he mounted and turned up the canyon.

"Know where we are?" Lucy queried.

He nodded.

"All right. I'll follow you."

The canyon climbed and they stayed with it until a side draw offered a trail to take them onto the ridge. Dale paused there, looking back, and heard the sounds he had been waiting for, in the canyon below. King Parson was still following.

He had no intention of letting his stepfather catch up. But he wanted the Thunderhead riders far back in the hills when darkness came, so that there would be that many fewer men guarding the herd.

The day wore on and the heat increased. Dale held their progress to a slow pace, partly to not outrun their pursuers too far, partly to conserve the horses for the night's work to come.

Twice during the afternoon they sighted the men on their back trail. Once the group came up close enough to send a useless shot echoing after the riders they pursued, and each time Dale cut away from them into the sheltering timber and led the girl to safety.

He was developing a dangerous contempt for these men who rode after them. There was no real effort on their part to flank them, no actual drive to attempt their capture.

The girl remarked on this just before dark as they rested their mounts on a high point above the deep canyon they had crossed.

Dale considered. "Maybe he isn't trying to catch us after all. I only saw four men the last time we had a glimpse of them."

Lucy looked at him questioningly. "Why do they keep following us then?"

"To keep us on the move; to keep us back in the hills. Maybe King out-foxed me after all. I planned to lead him away from the herd. Maybe he's letting us make ourselves do what he wants. From his point of view it's as good to keep us in the hills as it would be to lock us up in your house. We are out of his way. We can't warn the cattle buyers not to take your herd."

She stared at him. "Then we'd better go back to the valley."

"That's where we're going as soon as it's dark."

He mounted and led her on. At seven o'clock he dropped down into Shove Hill Canyon and found the trail he sought. This would lead them into the valley a couple of miles below her ranch house, close to where the trail to the pass started through the rock badlands.

He figured it would take them about two hours to reach the valley floor. It took three, and they came out onto the bench to look across the bedded herd. In the moonlight it seemed that the whole floor of the land below them was covered with cattle.

They were bedded down in a rough circle which must have been three or four miles across. Dale pulled up and sat looking out over them. Never in his life had he seen so many animals in one gather.

The girl at his side caught her breath. "It's impressive. I didn't know there were so many cows in the world."

He said soberly, "We're going to have trouble. This moonlight is too bright. The night riders are going to spot us before we come within half a mile of the bed ground."

She said, "What are you going to do?"

He was thoughtful. "We'll go in slow. Maybe they'll think we're some of their own men and we may get close enough to spook the cattle before they start shooting."

She pursed her lips, then said slowly, "There's another way."

He turned to look at her, hearing the note of consideration.

"What's that?"

"Fire the grass. The wind's blowing toward the herd, not strong enough to carry the fire fast, and the river should stop it unless the wind gets stronger."

It was a desperate act. Dale had all of the range

man's horror of grass fires, for although the spring grass was green and would hardly burn of itself, the winter mat of last year's late growth was still on the ground and would burn like tinder. The valley had never been over grazed, and the Colton range had always had more grass than the cattle would eat.

He said quietly, "It's your range."

She told him tightly, "I'd fire half a dozen ranges if it would stop King Parson."

Dale did not argue. He rode back into the timber, searching for what he wanted—resinous knots to be used for torches. When he returned he handed two to the girl.

"Let's go."

CHAPTER SEVENTEEN

The first fire he set died out before it got a good start, burning onto a bare spot and never coming to full life. The second caught in a dry clump of matted grass and flared up fiercely.

Dale and the girl had separated as they rode down slowly off the bench. Each moved forward quietly, trying not to startle the night riders who leisurely circled the bedded herd and sang to their charges.

Not until the first fire flared did anyone pay them attention. Dale was, he judged, within a quarter of a mile of the animals when he heard the line rider's high, wild yell of warning.

He rode grimly along the line he had mapped in his mind, halting every hundred feet to set a new blaze. The girl was riding in the opposite direction, and within minutes there were twenty fires blooming.

A rifle cracked, spurting dust at the feet of Dale's horse, making the animal shy. He twisted and saw that two of the riders had pulled away from the herd and were racing toward him.

He jerked his own rifle from the boot and took his time to drop the nearer rider. The other man reined up, turned and beat back toward the herd.

Dale continued calmly along his line, setting his blazes.

Behind him the small fires had spread and were creeping toward the bed ground, widening out to join together. Within five minutes there was a solid wall of flame head-high, pushing across the grass before a wind which seemed to be increasing.

The herd was lumbering to its feet, shifting uncertainly. No animal in the world is so unstable as a steer, so subject to sudden blind panic, and once he starts to run nothing will stop him except his own utter exhaustion.

Dale knew this well. He had seen gathers spooked by lightning, seen whole herds stampeded because one crazy steer was frightened by an odd-shaped bush and managed to transmit his panic to his fellows.

No, they would run, and the men set to guard them knew it as well as Dale did.

Some of the riders were attempting to mill the excited beasts, to start them moving in a circle, to start them away from the fire in orderly fashion. If they could get the cows to the river before the flames reached them they might avoid a stampede. Dale, however, had no intention of letting them succeed.

The fire was higher now, lighting the scene with a reddish glare, and the wind carried sparks and smoke before it. He turned after lighting his last blaze, satisfied with what he had accomplished, then rode directly toward the cattle. The critters had started to move but were not yet running.

Dale had no idea where Parson was. He saw that there were riders on point trying to keep the animals as bunched as possible, urging them toward the river which at this point was a shallow, lazy stream fifty to a hundred feet wide. None of the riders paid further attention to him. There was no one posted at the drag, since their problem was not to keep strays moving but rather to restrain the herd from gaining too much speed.

He came alongside the rear animals like a flying demon, shouting, flapping his hat with one hand, firing his gun into the air with the other. He saw the surge of quick fright catch the animals closest to him. He did not know and did not learn until later that Lucy Colton was performing the same routine on the far side of the vast herd.

The rear animals began to run, pushing those ahead of them, bellowing their fear and displeasure, butting a wave of panic through the massed pack until the leaders broke into wild flight. They charged for the river, the herd splitting, dodging the point men.

In seconds the gather had broken into as frantic a stampede as Dale had ever visualized. He pulled up, watching the herd run. The mingling smoke and dust rose in a roiling haze and made it difficult to tell exactly what was going on.

But he saw the leaders reach the river. Some veered along its bank but others, pressed by their fellows, plunged into the water, splashing, scrambling, bellowing.

Everything was turmoil. Dale saw a hundred scattered animals down. Some were calves knocked from their feet by the rush that spilled over them, some were cows weakened by the hard drive of the past few days. He rode among them. Some were dead, others at his approach struggled to their feet and took off weakly, tails high, after the herd.

He swung his horse, suddenly conscious that the fire was only two hundred feet behind him, its flames leaping out toward him, driven by the heightening wind. While he had paused to watch the stampede he had almost forgotten the burning grass. He twisted, quickly assessing how much of the herd was still on the near bank of the river. Cattle were piled up there. The water was filled with them, but most of the critters had managed the crossing and taken off, running for the distant hills with unbelievable speed.

He wondered how much tallow the stampede would take off the herd. Those that crossed the river safely would not stop running until they reached the security of the brush on the wide valley's far rim. There they would scatter into the canyons, making their way upward into the small mountain meadows where they were accustomed to summer graze. It would take weeks to comb them out of those hills—weeks that King Parson did not have.

King was beaten, there could be no doubt of that, and Dale was puzzled that the thought failed to give him pleasure. King was beaten, but at tremendous cost. The fat run off the herd would not be replaced fully by fall. Some animals around him were dead, others were dying in the shallow water of the river.

He turned and rode northward, looking for Lucy. The smoke was worse here, the fire closer. Its heat and small flying sparks blew against him as he called her name. And then he saw her, close to the river, still urging the last of the cattle into the water.

He started forward and, as he did so, three riders splashed across the shallow stream and surrounded the girl before she realized they were near.

Dale cursed and spurred his tired horse. Although he recognized King Parson as one of the captors, he dared not shoot, for his bullet could well hit Lucy Colton. He saw her fighting, striking out, then saw Parson range up beside her, grab her around the waist and lift her from her horse and carry her, still kicking, back across the ford.

The riders with Parson swung away, both firing at Dale as they turned. The first shot caught his horse in the neck. The animal screamed and reared, pawing wildly, and pitched over backward. Dale had one foot free of the stirrup as the animal went up, and he managed to shake himself loose, falling free as the horse collapsed.

He rolled away from the still thrashing hoofs and on his belly sighted his short gun deliberately and dropped the nearer rider. The second charged him, yelling, shooting as he came.

Dale dropped the horse scarcely twenty feet from where he lay, and saw the man fall and roll over and over and surprisingly come to his feet. Then he saw that it was Mark Jacoby, the Thunderhead foreman.

Dale scrambled to his knees and for an instant they faced each other. Then Jacoby rushed him. Dale shot and missed and the man was on top of him, beating at him with the heavy twelve-inch barrel of his gun. Dale weaved sidewise and the gun hit the point of his left shoulder, almost paralyzing his arm for the moment.

He dropped his own gun as Jacoby struck and, reaching out, caught the man's legs and dumped him onto his back. As Jacoby went down Dale scrambled forward, throwing himself across the heavy body. This was the man who, according to Old Coke, had killed both of his brothers. Dale's fingers reached for the thick throat and locked there with all the strength he had.

It was hard to see anything now. The smoke

211

had become dense. It stung his eyes, and the heat of the fire was very real. He could see only the leaping line of flames running toward him like the many tongues of a hungry monster, reaching to devour him.

Jacoby heaved, twisting his body, bringing up both hands to pry away Dale's strangling grip at his throat. He managed to break the hold, to roll out from under Dale, to spring to his feet. Dale had rolled also. Strength was coming back to his left arm and he set himself for the man's rush.

As Jacoby charged, arms swinging, Dale threw up his left forearm to block the wild flurry of punches, then drove a short, chopping blow against the side of the foreman's head. Jacoby went down, sinking to his hands and knees, one hand almost on Dale's gun. He grabbed it, started to raise it as Dale fell on top of him.

They lay there struggling without sound, Jacoby trying to twist the gun barrel against Dale's side, Dale fighting to keep it away. It was a struggle of sheer brawn, and out of the desperation that surged through him Dale found enough strength to bend the other's wrist, slowly, relentlessly, until the gun was against Jacoby's waist.

There was a sudden explosion, a heavy jolt which rang deafeningly in his ears. The man under him shuddered and was still.

For a moment Dale lay as he was, without the

strength to move and not knowing quite what had happened. His tortured lungs dragged in hot, choking smoke in their search for air.

He stirred groggily and rose to his knees, staring down at the figure below him. Jacoby was sprawled motionless on his back. The bullet had entered above the second rib, coursing through the body and literally tearing the heart out of the man.

Dale stood up slowly. He was conscious of a crackling noise which for a full minute did not register on his dulled senses. He turned vaguely, felt the heat of the fire against his face, and with a start became aware that his shirt was burning in two places, that the licking flames were hardly five feet from him.

The searing heat crisped his eyebrows and stung his skin. He stooped and caught up his gun, and then Jacoby's, hardly aware of his actions, and ran away from the fire toward the river. The smoke was so thick around him that he did not see the dead horse until he fell over it and slammed down on his bruised shoulder.

The heavy fall sent sharp splinters of pain knifing through him. His every impulse was to lie still, for he was so exhausted that the prospect of dragging himself back to his feet seemed beyond his capacity. But the instinct of survival finally brought him groggily to his feet and somehow he found the strength to stumble onward.

He did not see the river until he stepped off its two-foot bank headlong into the chilling water. The frigid contact of the water cleared his mind as he went under, and he came up sputtering, still holding the two guns, and stood in the waist-deep current.

The far shore was beyond his vision, but the noise of the fire sent him onward, splashing and struggling with not much more reason than one of the stampeded cattle. At the center of the stream he stepped into a deep hole and dropped over his head, but the heave of his body carried him forward and he found footing seconds later, thrashing onward until he reached the opposite bank.

There he sank down on the soft cushion of the grass, too whipped to venture further for the moment. He never knew how long he lay thus, but it could not have been more than three or four minutes. He sat up then, shaking the water from the guns and examining them. Jacoby's was empty. He knew now why the man had chosen to rush him rather than firing.

He had nothing to clean his own with, but he broke it and blew through the barrel. The smoke from the grass fire lay in a writhing pall around him, blotting out everything, even the moonlight. But he consoled himself with the thought that if he could not see, others could not see him.

He squatted there, listening, but the only sound

to reach his ears was the faint yet angry crackle of the fire on the other bank. He wondered dully if it would leap the stream and thought not. The wind was not that strong. But the urge to make certain drove Dale to his feet and he moved along the bank, looking for sparks or small fires which they might have started.

His action was one of instinct, for he was still not thinking clearly. Suddenly he stopped. The girl! He had forgotten Lucy and King Parson in the confusion of the last few minutes. Where was she? And where was King?

He stood listening. It seemed to him that the smoke was thinning slightly, as if the wind were carrying it off, and then he caught motion ahead of him in the gray fog and heard the movement of a horse.

For one crazy instant he thought it was King, still carrying the girl before him on the saddle. Then the rider loomed out of the smoke haze and he saw that it was not King.

The man was riding slowly, not looking toward Dale. He carried a wet blanket by one end and Dale guessed that he was patrolling the bank, looking for fires to put out in case a flying spark had jumped the water barrier and set a blaze on this side of the river.

The man was almost upon him now. Dale raised the gun, waiting until less than six feet separated him from the horse.

"Hold up."

The rider nearly jumped from the saddle. He dropped the blanket and his hand went down toward his gun.

"Don't try it."

The mounted man froze and sat motionless.

"Pull it slow and drop it," Dale ordered.

The man obeyed. He was staring at Dale as if he were seeing a ghost.

"All right. Get down and step back."

Again the man obeyed as Dale reached out with his free hand and caught the horse's reins.

"Where's King?"

"He took the girl back to the ranch house."

"How many with him?"

The man hesitated, wiping his mouth with the back of his hand. "He went alone. He said he wouldn't trust anybody else to guard her. He said he had to hold her until we could get the herd rounded up again."

"Where are the others?"

"Went after the cattle. He left me to see the fire didn't jump the stream."

"All right, you keep doing that, only on foot." Dale stooped and picked up the other's gun. He did not trust his own until it could be thoroughly cleaned. "I'm taking your horse." He swung up into the saddle.

The man watched him sullenly.

"You keep patrolling for fire. If it jumps the water I'll come back and kill you."

Dale reined the horse around then and rode carefully up the river, noting that the smoke thinned as he progressed.

CHAPTER EIGHTEEN

The headquarters of the IC ranch lay quiet and peaceful and apparently deserted under the hot sun. The acrid, oily smell of smoke hung in the air but no fire had reached the grass in this area.

The bed ground had been against a wide loop of the stream, so that the fire had been encompassed on three sides by water and there was small chance that it would burn back over the rocky bench against the wind, into the timber beyond.

Dale halted his horse on a low rise a quarter of a mile below the ranch yard and studied the place for signs of life. There were none, and he began to wonder whether the line rider had purposely sent him astray.

Even the cook shack showed no smoke, and the chuck wagon was gone from its open shed. Apparently King had not expected to come this way again, but to drive directly for the railroad from the bed ground.

He eased the horse forward, thinking that there would be no drive today, nor tomorrow nor the day after. Knowing King and the man's stubborn purpose he had no illusion that Parson had given up. Yet even with King in command it would take the combined crews days to comb the frightened cattle out of the brush. By that time Dale meant to have his own men and every mountain rancher he could persuade to ride with him ready to block the pass which lay across the route to the railroad, in the same manner as he had originally planned to block Squaw Canyon.

Meanwhile, the immediate problem was to rescue Lucy. There was, however, little he could do as long as King held her hostage. Once free, she could be sent to the railroad. Even if King should get through, she could warn the cattle buyers that every cow with the IC and a Thunderhead road brand were stolen animals.

He rode into the yard, swinging carefully past the blacksmith shop, the bunkhouse, the cook shack, the corral and sheds. There were no horses in the corral, but he took a sharp look at every building as he passed, for he had no stomach for riding into a trap.

At the porch of the main house he dismounted, looped the reins around a post and turned. There was a rifle in the boot and he pulled it free, making certain that it was loaded before he went silently up the three steps to the wide gallery.

There he paused again, listening, but nothing broke the stillness. The dust of the yard danced a little in the sun under the stroking of the light breeze. He had no real idea of the time except that the sun had not yet reached the zenith.

It had been long before daylight when he and

Lucy had started the fires, and it was impossible for him to gauge the passage of hours since then, although it must have taken him most of the forenoon to ride from the bed ground.

But where was King? Certainly Parson could have covered the same distance by this time, even with a horse carrying double.

Dale tried the front door gently, finding it unlatched, and then thrust it open, screening himself behind the jamb, thrusting the rifle into the opening.

Nothing moved in the shadowed hall beyond. The house had a deserted feel to it. He stepped inside, still not lured into rashness, and methodically searched through the rooms one after another. There was not a thing to indicate that King or Lucy Colton had been there that day.

Uncertainly he went back to the porch and scanned the valley below the house. The smell of the distant fire was still noticeable in the air, but there was no longer any sign of smoke.

And then he saw them, a long way off, not much more than a speck in the bright distance. He could not be certain that it was King and the girl. They were too far away. But he took no chances. Moving quickly down the steps, he untied the horse and led it across to one of the sheds and tethered it inside.

Then he came again into the sun, studying the yard with a sweeping glance, and decided on hiding in the house. If it were King, and he had the girl with him, they would probably ride directly to the porch as he had.

He went into the hall and shut the door. There was a small peephole window in its upper panel through which he had a restricted view of the steps and the beaten ground beyond them. He waited, the seconds ticking off in his head with maddening slowness.

He had about concluded that whoever he had seen was not headed for the ranch after all when, peering through the tiny window he saw the horse come wearily into the lower yard, almost staggering under its double burden. And as he had foreseen, King rode directly for the house, the girl motionless in the saddle before him.

They came up to the left of the steps and King swung down, reaching out to offer Lucy Colton his hand. She ignored it, sliding from her place and turning toward the steps, her head held high.

King started to follow her. It was Dale's plan to wait in the hall, his rifle held ready, to wait until the door was open, to shove the girl aside if she were the first, and drive the rifle into King's face.

But as he stepped down King's eyes had gone to the ground and picked up the tramped place in the dust where Dale's tethered horse, bothered by flies, had stomped restlessly. At once King was alert. The tracks were fresh, unclouded by the heavy dew of the preceding evening, and they told him as plainly as words that a horse had been tied here after the morning's sunrise.

He reached out, grabbing the girl with one hand, drawing his holstered gun with the other and Dale, who had seen the action and guessed its cause, cursed himself for his carelessness.

King jerked Lucy Colton back against his chest, wrapping his left arm around her waist so that her small body made an effective shield. The gun in his hand covered the door and his voice was flat and final.

"All right, Dale. Come out with your hands up or I'll shoot her now."

Dale hesitated. He could not shove the rifle through the peephole unobserved, and if he shot through the panel there was too much risk of the bullet warping enough to hit the girl. And he had no doubt that King meant exactly what he said. He had never been above murder and he had gone too far now to draw back. But Dale also knew that if he stepped through that door King Parson would probably shoot immediately.

He laid down the rifle and opened the door. Then, holding his palms out, shoulder high, he stepped onto the porch and slowly crossed it to the edge of the steps.

King glared up at him. Dale looked like a ghost out of another world. His clothes, burned in ragged holes by sparks from the fire, had dried on him and were wrinkled and dirty. His cheeks, sunken from the experiences of the last twenty-four hours were studded with a two-day growth of beard. He was hollow-eyed and muddy and he had lost his hat in the river crossing.

"You raised hell." There was a grudging note of admiration in King Parson's voice.

Dale didn't answer. There didn't seem to be anything to say.

"But you haven't beaten me." The voice turned savage. "Don't you know yet that nothing and no one ever beats King Parson. I'm going to kill you, Dale Thorne. I should have killed you the first morning you rode back to Thunderhead. That was my big mistake."

Still Dale did not answer. Had not the girl stood in the way he would have gone for his gun, even though King already had his heavy weapon in his hand. The chance was slim, but he might have succeeded in getting the bigger man even after King's bullet struck his body.

It would have been better. Anything would have been better than standing here like a clay pigeon, waiting for certain death. Dale Thorne had never been afraid of death, nor was he now. Yet it flashed through his mind that once he died Lucy Colton was equally doomed.

King certainly could not risk killing him and leaving her as an eye witness, a living finger to point to him at any time. Stealing the herd was one thing. He had the bill of sale he had forced

Lucy to sign, an element of legality to back up his actions if he had the mischance to be challenged. Murder was something else again. Murder had a way of following a man, haunting him all the days of his existence.

No, King would certainly kill Lucy, and Dale did not want her to die. Suddenly it flashed through his mind that he loved her. The realization came as a shock to him. He had been so preoccupied with his feelings for Clara that he had hardly considered Lucy as a woman.

But everything she had done bred a renewed admiration. She had never faltered, never whined or begged. It was ironical that he had to stand on the brink of death in order to understand what manner of woman she was.

He said quietly, "Think a moment before you pull that trigger, King." He had to stall—keep talking, do anything to put off even for seconds the crashing explosion of that heavy gun. "What have you got to gain by killing us? Do as you said, hold us prisoners here, or send us back into the hills with a couple of men for guards."

"That was before you stampeded the cattle."

"Then you're killing us for revenge."

"No," said King, "although I should. I'm killing you because I have no choice. You've scattered the herd so it will take weeks for us to re-gather it. I can't hold you prisoners that long. People are going to ask questions. Those men you've got collected in Squaw Canyon will come looking for you. I can't take the chance that they might find you, that you would lead them against me again."

Dale knew there was an axiom that a talking man seldom pulled a trigger, but he thought that this would not apply in King's case. King could afford to talk, even to gloat in his own way since the cards were obviously all in his hand. King held the gun and he held the girl, and there was nothing Dale could do about it.

But there was something Lucy Colton could do. Suddenly she twisted one hand free of King's grasping arm and caught the wrist of his gun hand, shoving it downward, throwing her whole weight sidewise, hooking her toe at the same time behind his knee in an effort to jerk him from his feet, shouting as she did so.

"Now, Dale. Now!"

She did not succeed in throwing King off his feet, but she did succeed in throwing him off balance and forcing the gun downward. As it exploded the bullet dug into the steps at Dale's feet.

He hardly heard the shot, for he had launched himself in a jumping dive which carried his body in a flying arc across the space between them.

King Parson was cursing harshly, trying to shake loose the girl's clutch on his gun hand. He cuffed her with his other hand, sending her sprawling, but in so doing he turned himself a quarter around. As he swung back to lift the gun again, Dale hit him with all the flying weight of his one hundred and eighty pounds.

King was carried stumbling backward. He lost the gun. Dale was on top of him, wrapping one arm around his neck, and they went down together, landing with a thud on the ungiving ground. Dale tried to keep his grip but the fall broke it, and King writhed to his knees, aiming a swinging blow which caught Dale on the right cheek and split the skin above the cheekbone.

He came in as King rose to his feet, diving from a crouch. His head caught the heavier man in the stomach, knocking him back, and again they went into the dust, again with Dale on top.

Lucy Colton lay where King's blow had spun her. Her eyes were open but she was so nearly unconscious that her nerve centers seemed to have lost all coordination, and she made no attempt to rise. Dale had a glimpse of her as he landed on the bigger man and for a moment thought she was dead, and the thought put added desperate power into the swinging blows which he rained into King's face.

All the fear and hatred so long stored within him for his stepfather fed the savage strength of his attack. However, though he was twenty years younger than King, the rancher was still a man of iron. He managed to arch himself and roll, dislodging his stepson and tumbling him onto his right shoulder. Then, with the quickness of a balanced cat, King was on his feet again and jumping for the gun in the dust beside the steps.

Dale caught him by one leg when he had almost reached the weapon and dragged him backward, and again they were locked in each other's arms, rolling over and over down the slight slope toward the bunkhouse and the corral below.

They did not stop until they hit the rear wall of the bunkhouse, and Dale found himself pinned between the stone foundation and King's burly body. He struggled to free himself, feeling King's rope-like fingers closing around his throat.

This struggle ran deeper than any fight for pure life. It was a battle that had been years in building, its roots in the boy's early resentment and fear, in the man's contempt for the boy. These two were as foreign as any two individuals could be. From the instant of the mother's remarriage King Parson had done everything in his power to humiliate the boy, driven by a sadistic urge to wipe out the image of the father he had supplanted as both owner of Thunderhead and husband.

Without warning King released his grip on Dale's throat and sent his left hand streaking toward the knife he carried in a special sheath stuck into the top of his boot. Sensing the nature of King's move, Dale hit him in the face. He got hold of the center finger of King's left hand and bent it backward until King was forced to let go of the knife before the bone snapped.

Then, his back against the wall, Dale used his knees in King's stomach to roll the man away, and came quickly to his feet. King rose more slowly, the knife now gleaming in his hand, its seven-inch blade outthrust as if it were a short sword.

Dale stood watching him, sucking air into his hot lungs. King was crouched a little, his big body bent forward, his eyes glittering as he took a slow step forward, measuring his intended victim, a half smile twisting his lips in anticipation of the kill.

Suddenly he lunged at Dale, slashing wickedly with the knife. Dale side-stepped desperately, the blade missing him by a bare inch. He seized the wrist and turned, and as he turned his boot heel caught on a half-buried root and he fell, dragging King down on top of him.

As they went over Dale lost his hold on the wrist, and with a savage grunting yell of satisfaction King stabbed him, once in the side, then a second time.

Dale felt no pain. His mind was so numbed by what he had been through that his nerve ends seemed to fail to react, but he knew that he had been stabbed. He grabbed the knife wrist with both hands and rolled, dragging the arm back until it almost pulled loose from King's shoulder.

A sharp cry of pain came out of Parson. He tried to break the lock on his wrist by wrenching his body to one side and succeeded only in rolling onto the point of his own knife.

For a long minute Dale did not even sense what had happened. He was so near exhaustion that it took real effort to raise a hand, to free himself of Parson's inert body. Then he turned the man over slowly and saw the knife handle standing out of the big chest, the blade completely sunk into the heart.

He fought slowly to his knees. He wiped the dirt and sweat away from his mouth. He clambered to his feet, felt the wet patch on his right side and stared blankly down at the blood blotting his shirt. For a time he thought the blood was Parson's, then he knew that it was oozing from his own two cuts, about an inch apart.

He pressed his hand over his side as if by so doing he could halt the bleeding, and began to stagger across the yard to Lucy who was just beginning to rise to her knees.

She saw him coming. She saw the blood, and suddenly the inertia which had held her loosened and she came up to her feet.

"Dale, what is it? Where are you hurt?"

He tried to answer her. He tried to bring up words from deep inside him but failed. He took a step toward her and then the world swam into blackness and he fell into a deep, bottomless pool that had no reality, no substance.

Lucy Colton ran toward him. She was not as a general rule a hysterical person, but the blow King had given her produced a condition closely resembling shock, and she had to fight for control.

"Dale!" She thought he was dead. She sat back on her heels, battling for the control she knew she must have. "Dale!"

He did not answer. His body remained utterly motionless. She bent over him and found that he was still breathing, and her natural capability took charge. She was used to violence and not shocked by the sight of blood. The first and most important task, she realized, was to stop the bleeding. There was no way to tell how deep the cuts were, how much blood he had already lost, or whether vital organs had been damaged.

And there was no help closer than Climax. She went quickly into the house for water and cloth to bandage Dale's side. She tied the bandage in place as tightly as she could, and saw it soak and redden almost as quickly as it was put in place.

There were no horses in the corral, but she found Dale's mount hidden in the shed and harnessed him, along with Parson's animal, to a buckboard. Neither horse had been broken to harness but both were too weary to give her much trouble.

Then she was faced with the problem of lifting Dale. He weighed a hundred and eighty pounds while she did not quite weigh a hundred.

She managed to drag him onto the porch steps, then backed the buckboard to them and somehow wrestled him aboard. Not until she had driven a full mile down the road toward Climax did she remember that she had neglected to look at King Parson, that she didn't know whether he was alive or dead.

CHAPTER NINETEEN

Lucy Colton's arrival in Climax created more excitement than the town had ever known. As she drove slowly in, her weary team barely moving, a crowd gathered about the buckboard, escorting her down the street to the doctor's office.

The doctor was a fussy man, long soured on both the country and his practice, and he shook his head as they carried Dale into his office.

"Waste of time. You should have left him lay."

She stood before him. She was dry-eyed and resolute. "He's not dead. He's still breathing."

The doctor snorted. "If you can call it breathing." He was watching Lucy closely. Like everyone in town he knew the full story of the Colton feud with Thunderhead. He had heard how she whipped Ford in the saloon, how she had carried Ford and Dale away as her prisoners.

"I call it breathing," she said. "You'd better save him, Doctor. I'm not fooling. If he dies because you don't give him proper care I'll run you out of this country."

She turned then and marched out of the room as if, having delivered Dale, she had no further real interest. She found a rider willing to go to Squaw Canyon and sent a message to Boyer to gather as many of the mountain men as he could and come to Climax on the run.

Then she went again to the doctor's office and stood by, watching him clean and then sew up the wounds.

Dale's face had a bluish cast. His breathing was irregular and very labored. Boyer found her there, sitting in a chair beside the bed, when he rode in at midnight.

"Is he going to make it?"

She said levelly, "He'll make it. Don't let that part worry you. Take your men and go after the crews. They're hunting the cattle. Parson is dead. Some of the boys rode out to the ranch this afternoon and buried him. Tell his crew that. I think they'll run. If they don't, drive them off the range."

She walked outside with him. He had brought nearly a hundred men, and they filled the street, silent and taciturn. She looked at them, then at Boyer.

"Keep them in hand. I want every Thunderhead man and what's left of my old crew out of the country. But there's been enough killing."

He did not quite meet her eyes. "I'll do my best, Ma'am, but some of the boys have taken a beating from Thunderhead for years. They've got long memories."

"So have I," she said curtly. "Just tell them that. Tell them I'll stand back of everything Dale

Thorne promised them. The valley will be open to anyone wanting to run cattle there, and those of you who want to work for me are welcome. I need a new crew. But if any man shoots one of the Thunderhead men unnecessarily, or if any of them are hanged, I'll find out who did it and I'll take care of him."

She swung back into the doctor's office. Boyer stared after her, whistling softly to himself. Then he turned to his horse and mounted. "That's some gal," he murmured.

The man beside him grinned. "Looks like Dale got himself a woman along with the ranch."

Boyer shrugged and pulled his horse around.

"Good looker."

"You can have her," said Boyer. "Me, I like them when they ain't quite so bossy. She's a little hard-shelled for me."

Inside the doctor's place Lucy Colton had gone to her knees beside the bed. Her small hand lay on Dale's hot forehead and for the first time there were tears in her eyes. Her whisper was choked as she said over and over, "You've got to get well, darling. You've got to."

Dale did not answer. He did not say anything for five days. Then he opened his eyes and the first person he saw was Lucy Colton, sitting in the chair.

He lay watching her, thinking her asleep, for her eyes were closed. He looked around the room, orienting himself, and then he went to sleep again and it was three hours later before she knew that he had finally regained consciousness.

When he wakened for the second time she told him gently what had happened. As soon as they had heard that Parson was dead, most of the Thunderhead crew had fled the range. Only two had put up a fight and they had been killed. Her own traitorous crew had faded into the mountains, glad to escape with whole skins.

Boyer and the Squaw Canyon men were gradually working the combined herds down onto the valley floor. There was nothing for him to worry about. King was dead. Dale was master of Thunderhead.

He listened. He was still terribly weak. He had lost a lot of blood.

"Now that I've brought you up to date on everything," she said, "I'm going to ride out to the ranch and see how Boyer is coming on. I'll be back tonight."

Dale reached out weakly and took her hand. "How did I get in here?"

"I brought you," she replied simply.

"Alone?"

She said almost fiercely, "You don't think I need help to handle one small man?"

He grinned a little and she turned quickly away so that he would not see the tears that again glistened in her eyes. She was so terribly relieved. She had about decided that he would never regain consciousness.

He was asleep before she closed the door.

When he next wakened Clara Austin was in the room. She saw that he was awake and came over and sank on her knees beside him, taking his hand in hers, tears running down her cheeks.

"Dearest. They wouldn't let me come to see you before."

"Who wouldn't?" His voice was hardly more than a whisper.

"That Lucy Colton." Her voice was outraged. "She knows that I love you, that it was my right to come and take care of you."

He blinked at her. This was the girl who had been going away with King. But King was dead. He had to remember that. King was dead and now he, Dale, had Thunderhead. That was why she was here of course. He wished he wasn't so weak. He wished he could think more clearly.

"Why wouldn't she let you come?"

"Because she wants you for herself."

That jolted him.

"But she can't have you, can she? I told her that. I told her you loved me, that you have ever since you came home." Clara's face was flushed and her eyes were like a warm caress.

"Clara!" It was Lucy, standing in the doorway,

a furious Lucy. Dale had never seen her so angry except on the night when she had whipped Ford in the saloon.

Clara turned. She came to her feet now, and she was as angry as the other woman.

"You've no right to order me around. You've no right to keep me out while you try to steal him for yourself."

"Clear out of here, you slut!" There was a short crop dangling from its loop around Lucy's wrist. She caught its handle suggestively. Anger shook her slender body and her glance struck Clara with the force of a heavy blow.

Clara backed away. "I know what you're doing." Her voice was stringent with rage. "You're telling him how you saved his life, how he wouldn't be here except for you."

"Get out." The short whip snaked out and almost struck Clara.

She ran. The door slammed and Lucy turned, still quivering with the intensity of her feeling.

"The little two-faced bum. She was all set to go away with King, and now, when she can't have him and the money from my stolen herd she has the nerve to come creeping back here. I'll kill her."

Suddenly Dale was laughing, weakly, laughing so that tears started from his eyes. Lucy stared at him in surprise. "What's so funny?"

He whispered, "Two women, fighting over me.

She said that you wanted me for yourself. Is that right?"

The anger was dying out of her. "I don't want any man who moons over a woman like that."

He said quietly, "I love you, Lucy."

"Why? Because you think you owe it to me? Because I dragged your carcass in here and saved your worthless life?"

He shook his head. "I knew it standing on the ranch porch, with King fixing to kill us both. That's what angered me, that I was going to die before I ever got a chance to tell you."

She looked at him for a long moment. The flush of wrath faded out of her face, leaving it startlingly white.

"I know you hate the Thornes and Thunderhead, but is there any chance, Lucy? Any chance for us?"

Her voice was almost a drawl, and suddenly she sounded amused. "I guess so, Dale. It's probably the simplest way. Our herds are so mixed up now it would take a Philadelphia lawyer to cut them out. The Thornes and Coltons started out as one outfit. I guess it's time to consolidate again." She came forward and bending over, kissed him gently.

Center Point Large Print
600 Brooks Road / PO Box 1
Thorndike, ME 04986-0001 USA

(207) 568-3717

US & Canada:
1 800 929-9108
www.centerpointlargeprint.com